THE LIZARD GARDEN

by

Anne Siglin

To Anna Grace
Happy reading!

Mrs. Siglin

Though this is a work of fiction, the story was inspired by the author's family and travels to the Netherlands.

Children of the Sea by Jozef Israëls
The Night Watch by Rembrandt van Rijn
Woman with a Child in a Pantry by Pieter de Hooch
(images used with permission by rijksmuseum.nl)

Edited by: Barbara Coyle and Carol B. Shell

Interior fonts: Times New Roman and Garamond
Art fonts— Trajan Pro 3 and Garamond
Cover photos: Julia Shepeleva /shutterstock.com
Max Topchii /shutterstock.com
Ekaterina V. Borisova /shutterstock.com
gillmar /shutterstock.com
Back cover image by Heidi Schmutzler

Connect with Me Online: annesiglin.com
Facebook: Anne Siglin, writer

Fiction/Youth/Mystery

Dedication

To Margaret and Elizabeth, who loved Ossenzijl with me and then helped me write about it.

Contents

1

The Lizards

"Amsterdam is as good as a TV show!" my little sister Alice exclaimed. She bounced up and down, attempting to peer into the window of a house. Mom snatched her back.

"Just because there aren't curtains on the windows doesn't mean you can be rude, Alice," she scolded. "The families who live here are not television shows to watch."

"Oh, I don't know," my older brother Milo said. "They can't mind too much, or they'd cover up the windows. And Alice is right. It really is like TV." He pointed toward the row of houses that fascinated Alice. "Sitcoms and dramas right over there. And go over this direction," he said, gesturing toward the arched bridges and church spires along the canal, "and you've got the National Geographic Channel. I think it's awesome."

Milo might as well be practicing to work for the National Geographic Channel. He's already shot miles of video of Dutch canals and has a photo to show for almost every five steps he's taken. His goal is to print out the pictures and string them together in one long, watery map and make a book. Milo is smart. It's a pretty good idea, even if I'm not going to admit that to him, but Alice and I still like looking inside the houses best.

At twelve, I'm old enough to know I shouldn't look in other people's windows, but today I did it anyway. Some of the rooms seemed deserted, as if life inside them just paused until the owners came home again. But in others, I saw people going about their day. A mother in one house read picture books to her little boy. In the next, a man worked on a laptop at a dining room table, and in the third, a grandmother smiled and sang as she watered dozens of houseplants.

All the houses have something in common, besides spotless windows. They're personal and full of life, with plants and pictures, funky modern art on the walls, beautiful blue dishes, or rows of books. You can tell what kind of people live in them just by looking inside. Our house isn't like that at all.

If you peeked inside the windows of our apartment in Boston, you'd hardly get any clues about our family. Because of Dad's job, we move every year, and neither of my parents bother much with the kinds of things that make a house look lived in or cozy. Mom says it's too much work to put much on the walls only to take it all down a few months later, so she keeps things streamlined. We can pack up and move to a new house in about a week, and when we leave, there aren't any holes in the walls. Well, except in the entry, which will have about twenty neat little patches left over from Mom's family picture wall.

There's always a big photograph of the five of us in the middle of the wall, and around that Mom arranges smaller ones of all our grandparents, aunts and uncles, including the ones on Dad's side of the family that we've never met. One of the first things we see at a new house is Mom, hammer in hand, hanging up the family pictures.

"We may not spend much time with them," she mumbles through a mouthful of nails, "but family is important. I don't want you kids to forget who these people are."

There's one picture I especially love. It was taken years ago at Grandma Sybil's birthday party, right before Grandpa died. Milo was eight and I was seven, and even back then he was about a foot taller than me. I inherited the same short gene Mom and Uncle Jack got, and I got their dark hair too. In the picture, Milo is standing next to our cousin Anthony, looking annoyed, probably because Anthony just poked him. Alice is a perfect, blonde, curly-haired baby sitting on my lap. Her arms are thrown out and she's hamming it up for the camera. She still does that, even though she's the same age I was then. In the picture I'm hugging Alice with one arm, and my other arm is around my cousin Annabeth. We look like sisters, and we've always been best friends. My parents are both laughing, probably because of something funny my dad said, and my aunt and uncle and grandparents are laughing too. When I look at the picture, it makes me feel warm and happy, like I always do when we're together.

They all live in Fraser, Missouri, a little town right outside of Kansas City. I lived there too last year, during fifth grade. I saw my cousins, Aunt Tracy, Uncle Jack, and Grandma Sybil all the time, at least every week at church. It was the best year of my life, but it couldn't last forever, and when it was over Dad took a new contract in Boston.

I always cry a little bit when we move because I hate having to change houses and make new friends all over again. But the day I found out Dad had a new job and we would be leaving Kansas City in a month, I slammed the door to the room I shared with Alice, dove under the bed, and refused to come out for two hours. Not that crying did any good, and I couldn't even do that in peace. Alice, who still believed dust bunnies might be real, kept pulling on my foot and yelling at me not to disturb the rabbits under there. Dad came in and sat down on Alice's bed.

"I'm sorry, Charlotte," he'd said that day. "I know it's harder to move this time because of the family here, but we'll still visit and call and stay in touch. That's a priority.

We always did that before and we'll do it again. But this job in Boston is too good of an opportunity to pass up. We need to go where the money is, and my contract here is finished."

"But it's different this time, Dad," I said, crying. "Everybody important is here. We finally really belong somewhere, and we never did before. I know when we came you said it would only be for one year, but I really thought you and Mom would find a way to stay. Especially Mom. What does she say about Boston?"

I could only see Dad's feet, but by the way they shifted around when I mentioned Mom's name, I got the distinct impression that she might not like the idea of moving any more than I did, and maybe he'd just finished delivering the same pep talk to her.

Mom's eyes looked red at dinner that night, but she talked brightly about Boston and how much fun it would be to live near the ocean and visit Old North Church, and Lexington and Concord. The next weekend the two of them flew to Massachusetts to find us a place to live, and pretty soon she kicked into gear and started dealing with the move the way she always did, by planning homeschool units and ordering books. For our Boston year we studied marine biology and the American Revolution.

A few months ago, she ordered another big stack of books, because of course we're moving again. Dad's new contract will be in Oregon. Judging by the contents of the boxes from Amazon, when school starts for us in September, we'll be learning about mountains, pioneers, and the Westward Expansion.

Though we've lived all over the United States, my parents have always wanted to take us to Europe, so when a company here in the Netherlands offered Dad a contract for the summer, they jumped at the chance. Mom made sure to bring a suitcase full of books for us to read while we're here, too, about William the Silent, tulips, the Dutch Resistance during World War II, and of course, windmills. We already know a ton about windmills, since Dad works as a wind turbine engineer. Art history is his hobby, though, so Mom also brought books about Rembrandt, Vermeer, and Vincent van Gogh.

Although Dad has to work a lot during our trip, today he showed us Amsterdam. He knows it well, since he comes here a few times a year for meetings. One of his favorite places in the world is the Rijksmuseum, which is full of famous Dutch art. Every time Dad visits, he brings each of us kids a postcard, and tells us a little bit about his favorite paintings from that trip. I'm looking forward to seeing my postcard paintings.

Last year, though, Dad discovered something amazing outside the museum. He says it's spectacular, and that we'll absolutely love it. He refuses to give any hints except that it's not too far from the museum, in a park called the Leidesplein.

"I bet it's the Apple store!" Milo said eagerly. Milo loves computers and technology of all kinds.

"Milo, you could go to the Apple store anytime," Dad said. "We've been there over and over. This is ten times better than that." Milo frowned. He didn't see how anything could be ten times better than the Apple store.

My own idea of a perfect surprise would be a store with things to make. If I could own a Dutch shop, I would sell interesting things, maybe plain wooden shoes you could decorate at tables in the back. Or I'd have about a thousand kinds of beads to make necklaces and bracelets. The whole store would smell like coffee and hot chocolate, which you could buy to drink while you worked, and maybe there would be cupcakes too. But that would never be Dad's secret. He likes cupcakes and coffee well enough, but he doesn't do crafts and he hates to shop.

Alice grabbed Dad's hand. "It's a zoo! Please tell me it's a zoo, Daddy," she pleaded, jumping up and down. "A zoo, only all the animals are babies, and it's safe to pet them. With a little fence around the whole thing, to keep them safe." Alice thinks about animals every waking minute.

"You're on to something, Alice," Dad said, grinning and swinging her hand so hard she had to run back and forth to stay connected. "Your idea is the closest, anyway. We're almost there."

We crossed another bridge to an area crowded with shops and restaurants. "Watch your purse, Charlotte," Mom called back to me. "And walk a little faster. This street is a pickpocket's dream."

She was right. I put my hand tightly over the zipper of my bag and pushed through the crowd to keep up. We passed a McDonalds, some Dutch pancake restaurants, and a store selling beads, almost like my dream store. I didn't ask to stop, though, because Dad was in a hurry for us to get to wherever we were going. We turned the corner, and Dad didn't need to say anything. Clearly, we'd found his surprise.

I stood staring for a minute, and then burst out laughing. So did Mom. Milo's mouth dropped open, and then a huge smile spread over his face. He gave Dad a high five. "Way better than the Apple store," he said, and they laughed together.

Alice began to squeal. She let go of Dad's hand, darted across the sidewalk, and in about ten seconds she had thrown her arms around the biggest lizard I've ever seen.

2

Apocalypse

I blinked and looked again. All across the lawn of the tiny park, lizards perched along the brick fence and grazed in grim bronze contentment. When I looked a second time, I could see that none of them were real. I started to count but there were too many. Milo told me later that he quit when he got to thirty. Alice yanked up grass by the handfuls and blissfully pretended to feed her new friend. "Her name is Bambi," she yelled to Mom. "I just love and love her!"

"It's like a zombie apocalypse," Milo crowed. "Dad, get a picture of me shaking in terror. My friends at home are gonna think it's great." Dad snapped half a dozen pictures of Milo and some of Alice darting from lizard to lizard, and then one of Mom and me outside the fence, laughing. Dad came over and put his arm around Mom, who was shaking her head. "Oh, Jeremy, this place is so *you*," she said, and he grinned.

"Years ago an old sea captain retired here and kept a miniature zoo in the courtyard of his pub," he told us. "I doubt the animals were all as friendly as Alice would have liked, or we wouldn't still know about him. A few years ago the city sponsored an art competition to spice up the park and this was the design that won. It's named *Blauw Jan* in honor of the old captain. Brilliant, isn't it? No two statues are exactly alike. And they each have such personality."

He pointed to a set of lizards with long necks and powerful, whip-like tails, who stared at each other as lovingly as creatures with little marble-y eyes possibly could. "Look, Meg," he said. "I think those two are husband and wife. They could be us, don't you think?"

Alice hopped over the fence and ran over to me. "Can I have some post-it notes and a pen?" she asked. "Charlotte, will you be my secretary? I'm giving them all names, but there are so many, and I'm afraid I'll forget who is who. So I want to label them. This one is Steve." She patted a convenient lizard's head. "And that one is Chummy. That one is Melissa, and I think that one over there looks a little like Uncle Jack, so that's his name..." Alice reeled off half a dozen more names before I could stop her.

"Alice, we can't put labels on them," I protested. "But if you want, I'll write down some of the names for you so you don't forget." I fished a pen and a notebook from my purse and then trailed around the park behind Alice, recording names for her. Alice can write, but her mind is about a hundred miles ahead of her fingers, and there were lots of lizards to name. We hadn't gotten through half of them before Dad called us back.

"Glad you like these fellows, but we need to get to the museum. I want to get our money's worth before we head back to the rental house in a few hours. You'll be back here again, I promise. No, Alice, you can't kiss them all goodbye."

We pulled Alice out of the park, and she waved to the lizards until she couldn't see them anymore. She talked about Violet, Twigs, Persephone, and the others all the way to the museum. Fortunately we didn't have far to go.

Mom and Dad never feel like they can take a break from teaching us things. Most of the time I don't mind, although Milo likes to pretend he already knows everything they're about to tell him. It drives them crazy and me too, sometimes. I was afraid we would go through the museum room by room, with Dad lecturing us on the various artists and their time periods, and frankly, I've been dreading that even though I like art. But Dad surprised me.

He handed Milo and me our tickets, and told Alice she'd have to stay within sight of one of us. The Rijksmuseum offers a treasure hunt for kids, and the lady at the desk passed Alice a clipboard with the English version.

"Go through and answer these questions," she told us, "and when you're finished, come back here and I'll check your work. The prize is a free postcard if you find everything." She peered at Milo through glasses on a chain. "Would you like a treasure hunt too?"

Milo wrinkled his nose. "Um, no. I'm fourteen." After receiving a sharp glance from Mom, he quickly added, "But, um, thank you ma'am, for asking."

"We'll meet you back here in an hour," Dad said. "Mom and I are going to spend some time in the Rembrandt room upstairs. I'm sure we'll run into you there. Right? And remember what I told you earlier. I'll give you a Euro coin if you can find the picture that matches the postcard I brought you last fall. Tell me something new about the picture that you didn't see in the postcard." I should have known we wouldn't get off without him packing extra education into this experience.

Milo took off by himself. Alice skipped beside me and put her hand in mine. "I'll stay with you, so we can fill out our treasure hunt together, and find Daddy's pictures. Do you still have our postcards in your bag?" I rummaged around and pulled them out. The postcards were a little beat up from the bag and from being taped to our bedroom wall since last September.

I'm not like Mom. When we move, I put posters and pictures and even stuff like Dad's postcards all over my bedroom wall. So does Alice. Mom sighs and claims there is no visual resting space in our room, but she doesn't make us stop. I handed Alice the postcard.

"Here. Jozef Israels. *Children of the Sea.*"

Alice studied it for the thousandth time. "It's us when we were little, I think," she said after a few moments. "Milo is carrying me on his back. You're the girl playing with the toy boat. The extra girl is Annabeth." Alice likes Annabeth almost as much as I do. "Can I look at yours, Charlotte? I want to see it again." I passed it to her.

I love my picture. It's a mother and child, by an artist named Pieter de Hooch. I completely messed up the pronunciation of his name when I first read it on the back of the postcard, but Dad corrected me and said it should rhyme with oak. After that it was easy. I know why he thought I would like it. The woman in the picture looks like Mom, and her little girl could be Alice. It's almost like I'm standing a few feet away, watching the two of them like I have a million times, and somehow I feel like I'm part of the scene even though I'm not in the picture. In my imagination, I'm wearing a dress in my favorite dark red, with a stiff lace collar and a skirt to my ankles. I just know it twirls perfectly.

The little girl from long ago has bright golden hair and looks every bit like the Dutch girl Dad teases Alice that she is. Our last name is Smith, but Dad says that a long time ago, before his ancestors came from the Netherlands to America, it used to be Smit. It's the reason he is always extra happy to visit here.

We found my painting almost right away, since it was in the same room with the two enormous dollhouses that Alice insisted we see first. She climbed the ladder in front of one of them and started assigning everyone in our family his or her own room. Once she was settled there, I turned around to my picture.

It was perfect. The color, the light—just everything glowed, and I wanted to laugh because the walls in this house were bare, too, except for one lone family picture over by the window, and the house had barely any furniture. Did this family keep their belongings pared down so they could move in a hurry, like we do?

That's what I planned to report to Dad, but I noticed other things about the real painting that I hadn't seen on the postcard, like the beautiful detail on the little girl's cap and her bright and shining blonde hair. I wanted to remember those things too. I pulled my journal out of my bag. It's kind of heavy, but I take it everywhere on the trip with me so I can draw and write things down.

Before we left Boston a week ago, I got a package from Annabeth. It was a journal she'd decorated herself. I could tell it had started out as a big blank book, but she'd covered it with dark blue flowered material that looked old, like a Dutch tile, with a striped border around the edges. She sewed on a button and a ribbon to keep it closed. Inside the journal, she drew boxes with dates for each day and left space for me to draw a picture and write a little bit. I called Annabeth to thank her for the journal.

"Well, don't waste this trip," she lectured. "Everyone in books who goes to Europe takes notes or draws pictures. You should too. What if you're important someday? Your biographers will want a record. And even if you aren't famous, you'll want to tell your grandchildren about it. And even if they aren't interested, I'm going to be. So you better not forget a single thing."

"Yes, Ma'am," I said, laughing. So far I haven't missed a day. I don't dare. I reached into my purse again and took out my favorite blue pen.

There was no bench in the gallery, but since nobody

but Alice and I were there, I sat down right on the floor to draw. Fortunately, Alice can look at dollhouses forever, so I had time to make a decent picture, and I made a diagram of where it was on the wall and wrote down a little bit about the pictures on either side. I was so intent on my journal that I didn't even hear Milo come into the room behind me until he started reading my entry out loud, in a high-pitched voice with his nose pinched shut.

The house in the picture intrigues me. I wonder who the man in the portrait on the wall is. He looks about the same age as the lady. Did her husband die and leave her the teapot that she's showing the little girl? Or is the picture of her grandfather when he was younger?

My words coming out of Milo's mouth sounded completely ridiculous, and the peaceful moments I'd just spent drawing and writing felt silly and spoiled. I forgot I was in one of the most famous museums in Europe. I jumped to my feet and grabbed Milo's arm. Alice turned around on the ladder and watched through the rungs with interest.

"Get away from me, Milo!" I almost shouted, barely scaling my voice back after the first word, once I realized how amazing the acoustics were. But Milo had memorized my next line and whispered it back to me with a maddening smile on his face. *"He looks really stern. I'm glad he's not my dad. Oh, Charlotte, this is fascinating. Let me read the rest."* He made a grab for my journal, and I ran for the door. Unfortunately, Mom was right there and she looked furious.

"Really, kids? You're fighting *here?*" Her whole face was red. She was definitely thinking about things like acoustics, and maybe hidden cameras, since her next words came out in a hiss. "Done. Over. We'll be talking about this later. Milo, find Dad and stay in the same room with him. Girls, you come with me."

"*I* didn't do anything, Mommy," Alice said in her sweetest voice, as she climbed down the ladder. I trailed along behind, still mad at Milo. I stuffed the journal back in my bag.

We spent another hour in the museum. Milo sat on a bench blowing bubbles with his gum most of the time, and I avoided him as much as possible. I knew we'd get in trouble the minute we went out the door or at least on the train on the way back to the rental house. I tried to think ahead to when it would all blow over, and we'd be back home.

The rental house had felt like home right away. It has a thatched roof a foot thick, books and pictures everywhere, and even a window seat between the two upstairs bedrooms. There are bikes in the shed, and best of all, a rowboat and canoes to use on the canal right behind the house. We were barely willing to leave it to come to Amsterdam. I knew that when we got back, Milo would want to take the rowboat, but I decided to let him. I would do the smart thing and help Mom. It might put her in a better mood, and maybe she'd forget our bad behavior faster.

But I didn't get the chance to help, and we didn't get punished. On the way out of the museum, Mom turned her cell phone on, and it buzzed angrily. When she saw seven texts from Uncle Jack pop up on the screen, one after another, her face wasn't red like when she'd been mad at us earlier. It went completely white.

3

Dutch Summer

Nobody said a word as Dad guided us over to a bench near the museum entrance. The lacy-looking bench would have been the perfect place to take a family picture to hang with the others on our wall back home. Now it would be the perfect place to get horrible news. Who was sick or dead? Aunt Tracy? Grandma Sybil? Anthony? Annabeth. *Oh please, not Annabeth*, I prayed silently, and then immediately felt guilty. I wanted everybody to be okay.

Dad put his arm around Mom and squeezed her. "Do you want me to make the call?"

She shook her head. "No, I'll do it." She took a deep breath and dialed Uncle Jack's number. I don't think it rang more than once before he picked up. I tried to lean closer to Mom to hear better, but she frowned a little and leaned away from me, and I only caught a word or two. Something about "Mama" and "a diagnosis." It was Grandma Sybil then. But a diagnosis of what? I don't know too many people healthier than my grandmother.

When Grandma Sybil came to visit us in Boston, we took her to the Boston Common, and the Public Gardens, and the Old North Church. But the main thing she came for was to run the Boston Marathon. I hate running...or any exercise, really. I can barely make it around the block without getting out of breath, but Grandma loves to run and enters races all the time. Sometimes she even wins in her age category. She says that when she turns seventy-five, she'll scale back on running and take up yoga instead, but I don't believe it. She's seventy-four now but she looks ten years younger, and she's always trying to get Mom to quit cooking so much red meat and give up butter and sugar. How could Grandma Sybil be sick enough for Uncle Jack to call us in Europe?

Alice whimpered a little bit and even Milo, who heard about as much of the conversation as I did, looked stricken. Mom clicked the phone off and looked up at us. She sighed and wiped her eyes with the back of her hand.

"Grandma Sybil has cancer. It looks like they found it early, but she's having surgery to remove the tumor next week, and she'll need chemotherapy treatments every week for most of the rest of the summer. Uncle Jack and Aunt Tracy both have their jobs, so I need to get to Kansas City as soon as I can. And I guess you kids are going to have to come with me."

Now Milo looked really upset. He loves being here. We all do. I felt terrible about Grandma Sybil, but selfishly I didn't want this trip to be over so soon.

"Wouldn't it be easier for you to take care of your mother if the kids stayed here with me?" Dad asked. "Who's going to watch them while you're at the hospital? And when she gets home, she'll be feeling rough. If I were her, I'd want a quiet house."

"Well, who's going to watch them over here?" Mom asked. "You'll be working all day and coming into Amsterdam once a week. I don't want the children roaming the countryside by themselves. I can just picture Milo taking off on an adventure and finding himself in Belgium or Germany without a passport, and Charlotte with a wrecked bike by the side of a road, miles from the house, or Alice at the bottom of the canal." She looked from one to the other of us, indignant, and I giggled, since I could picture any of those things happening. In Mom's mind, they already had.

"Admit it, Jeremy," she said. "When you're working, you're in another world, even if you're in the next room." Dad looked guilty, but unfortunately he couldn't deny this. So we tried to make her feel better.

"I'll wear my life jacket, I promise!" insisted Alice. "I'll never go near the water without it."

"I'll keep track of Alice, Mom," I said. "I'll help Dad with the chores, too."

"Charlotte can use the best bike all the time so she won't wreck," Milo offered. "I'll even fix it so it fits her better." I turned around to see if this was really Milo speaking, or the older brother I'd always dreamed of having. But it was definitely Milo. "And we'll do whatever Dad says," he added.

"That would be a first," Mom said.

"We will obey Daddy," Alice insisted. "We'll be very, very good. You should go help Grandma by yourself."

I thought about sitting in Grandma Sybil's house in Kansas City while she and Mom were at the treatment center, with nothing to do except bicker with Milo and Alice. Grandma Sybil thinks air conditioning is an unnecessary frill, and that the oak trees around her house keep it from ever getting really hot. Nobody else agrees, but we don't have to live there. I love Grandma Sybil's conversations and I love going places with her, but I don't always love every minute of visiting her house. She serves Grape Nuts for breakfast and makes tofu stir fry for supper, and we only get fruit for dessert.

Mom gave us a pitying smile. "I know you'd have more fun here, and there wouldn't be much there for you to do but sit in the house and worry about Grandma, especially since Annabeth and Anthony are in day camp all day."

Her mind swung from Europe to America and back again. She turned around and looked severely at Milo.

"Not an hour ago, you and your sister had an outrageous scene in a public place. Who knows what would have happened if I hadn't come in just then? How can I possibly consider leaving you three?"

Milo gulped, sat a little straighter, and said, "I'll make sure it doesn't happen again. Really, I don't want you to worry. Worry about Grandma Sybil, but don't worry about us. We're going to be fine."

There was my perfect brother again, but he sounded like he really meant it, and Mom smiled at him through her tears.

"It makes me feel good to hear you say that, and I know you mean it, at this moment at least. I just hope..." She took a deep breath, made her decision, and turned to Dad. "OK, let's book my ticket to Missouri. I know I'll regret this, but..."

She didn't have time to finish this sentence because her phone rang, and this time it was the little piano riff that told us Grandma Sybil herself was calling. Mom's hands shook as she answered it.

"My son Jack is dead meat!" Grandma Sybil shouted. None of us needed to lean close to hear *this* conversation. "You and Jeremy have wanted to take the kids to Europe since Milo was *born*. This is your opportunity, and Meg, I'm not going to have you come back here to play nursemaid to me. I'm perfectly capable of taking care of myself. Didn't Jack tell you they caught it early? It's barely cancer at all yet!"

"Mama," Mom began, but she might as well have saved her breath because Grandma Sybil talked right over her.

"The surgery is nothing, Meg, no big deal. Jack or Tracy can take off a couple days of work, and after that I'll be fine. The doctor says I'm in such great shape that it's hardly going to be a bump in the road. And only six weeks for treatments after that. He promised. Six weeks is hardly anything! I can drive myself a few miles, sit there and read a magazine while they pour the poison in and be back home in time for lunch every day."

That very minute, I stopped worrying about Grandma Sybil. She'd be fine, but she wouldn't go to those treatments alone. Everything Mom knows about being stubborn, she learned from Grandma Sybil. Mom went straight from sad to mad.

"Mama, stop being ridiculous," she snapped. "I'm coming home to be with you, as soon as I can get there. Jeremy and the kids will stay here together. That's it, that's final, that's how it's going to be."

There was another stream of yelling from Grandma Sybil. Dad reached over and took the phone out of Mom's hand.

"Sybil, Meg is coming," he said. "Either she comes alone or she brings all the kids with her, and I think it's going to be better for everyone if they stay here. Of course you could handle this by yourself, you're the strongest woman I know, but we don't want you to be alone." I could hear Grandma Sybil hollering again and Dad put up his hand like a policeman, as if she were here with us and could see him instead of four thousand miles away. Strangely enough, it worked.

"You and I both know you don't really want that either, no matter what you say," Dad continued. "So Meg is coming. She'll be there as fast as we can get the ticket arranged. I love you, Sybil, and I'm glad they caught this early. You'll be back to your running club by fall, I bet."

It was still quiet on the other end of the line, and I think it was Grandma Sybil's turn to cry. Mom may be her daughter, but she and Dad love each other a lot, and they understand each other. He can say things to her that Mom or even Uncle Jack would never get away with. Dad passed the phone back to Mom, who got up from the bench and walked down the path by herself to finish the conversation.

"Thanks, kids," Dad said. "This is going to be rough for all of us, but we're going to make it work."

He sounded confident, but I'd begun thinking about all the things that Mom does that we would have to do. Realistically, I knew a lot of the work of running the house would fall to me, and suddenly, sitting at Grandma's in Kansas City didn't sound like such a bad idea, especially if Milo and Alice stayed here. I could at least see Annabeth at night and possibly stay with her on weekends. Maybe I should go with Mom. Cleaning up after her and Grandma Sybil would be easy compared to cooking and cleaning up after the rest of the family.

And then there was Alice. If I stayed here, she'd trail after me and only me the whole summer. I started to volunteer to make the sacrifice to go with Mom, but it was too late. Dad was thinking just one step faster than I was and had already connected all my dots. He put a hand on my shoulder.

"Charlotte, no way could I manage without you or Milo. Either you all go with Mom, and you help there, or you all stay here and help here."

So I guess it will be a Dutch summer after all. We'll be eating a lot of pancakes. I hardly know how to make anything else.

4

The Rowboat

It took two hours to get from Amsterdam back to the rental house. During the train ride, Mom's pen flew as she made list after list—things to take along with her to Missouri, things for us kids to do that would hopefully keep us busy and out of trouble, and chore assignments to keep things running smoothly after she left. She had to write around Alice, who was squashed into the same seat with her even though there were plenty of empty ones around them. Alice didn't say much during the ride and sat with her arms folded and her lips pressed into a straight line. She's never been apart from Mom for more than a night or two. Taking care of the usual fun-loving Alice was going to be enough of a challenge. Taking care of a homesick-for-Mom Alice might be even harder, even if this Alice was quieter.

We changed trains once, and when we got to the town of Steenwijk, we got off the train and walked over to the bus stop. The local bus is really just a van. The village we're staying in, a little town called Ossenzijl in the northern part of Holland, is too small to have a real bus. If our whole family needs to go somewhere together, we just have to hope nobody else is riding. Last week, when we came straight from the airport, the bus driver had to phone for an extra van for us and all our suitcases.

After spending the day in Amsterdam, the countryside seemed strange and new again. There was no trash on the streets, and the people looked sensible and tidy. So did the farmland and small villages. When the driver stopped to let someone off, I smelled freshly spread manure. I didn't mind that too much, though, since it reminded me of driving in the country outside Kansas City.

Alice paid no attention to the scenery we rode through. Instead, she doodled houses on the back of the Rijksmuseum treasure hunt. She drew long, skinny rectangles with tiny triangles on top to look like Amsterdam canal houses. To make country farmhouses, she turned the rectangles sideways and stuck enormous triangles on top. I bet the attics of the real farmhouses are so big you could ride bicycles in them.

The houses may look different here, but both city and country houses have big, plate-glass windows in the front room, and they're so clean they look like mirrors. If the windows have curtains at all, it's just a ruffle of lace along the top. You can see right into the farmhouse living rooms, just like the Amsterdam living rooms, and inside the window each housewife has made a little decorated display, with plants, art, or anything else she deems pretty. I'd like to decorate a window like that.

When we finally got home, Mom immediately began packing for her trip. Later, after dinner, we tried to do some of the things we've enjoyed doing since we arrived last week. We made coffee and hot chocolate, shared a big Dutch chocolate bar, and watched a DVD. Dad chose Jeeves and Wooster, Mom's favorite show, about a rich British bachelor named Bertie Wooster who's always getting himself into ridiculous situations only to be saved by his much smarter butler, Jeeves. We usually laugh and laugh when we watch Jeeves and Wooster. But tonight nobody did, and we quit watching right in the middle of an episode so Mom could put Alice to bed.

She took much longer than usual doing it. I went to

our room to get my pajamas before I took my shower and found Mom lying on the bed next to Alice. They talked about the peaceful field across the canal, about the friendly ponies we see on the way to the grocery store, and the ancient, ruined farmhouse just barely visible from the bedroom window. Alice was almost asleep and not really paying attention to the conversation.

But Mom was, and listening to her talk, I knew she would miss these things and so many others after she left us. I tried not to think how much I was going to miss her being with us, too. I've been away from Mom and Dad for a week or so at Grandma Sybil's or Annabeth's house, but those times my parents were either in the same city with other relatives or a short plane ride away. Tomorrow Mom would be all the way across the Atlantic Ocean, and I wouldn't see her for weeks. Somehow I wanted to tell her I'd miss her as much as Alice would, but I couldn't make the words come out, and I got my things to take my shower without saying anything.

The next morning, we stumbled out of bed really early so Mom and Dad could catch the first bus back to the train station. Alice cried when they left, but not too much. Even she could see that Mom was having a hard time, and I was proud of her for trying. I squeezed her hand and she squeezed mine back.

"I'm afraid I'm going to go through all my Kleenex before I even get to the bus," Mom said, wiping her eyes as she hugged me. "I don't want to leave any of you."

"We're going to be fine," Milo told her, standing very straight. "We'll all behave ourselves and help Dad." He sounded as sincere as he did yesterday and she smiled.

We don't have a car here, so Mom and Dad walked the mile to the bus stop, dragging the suitcase behind. We could hear the bump, bump from her wheeled bag all the way down the brick-paved road. Ossenzijl is so flat that you can see for a long way, just like you can in Kansas City, but finally they disappeared past the trees that lined the lane and we couldn't see them anymore.

Feeling subdued, we went back into the house and closed the door. Milo drifted toward Dad's computer. I thought Alice might burst into real tears now that she could do it without upsetting Mom, but she didn't. She wiped her eyes with the back of her sleeve, gulped a few times, and then tugged at my arm, pointing to the list Mom had left on the table.

"What are we supposed to be doing right now?" she asked.

I picked it up. "Let's see. Well, according to Mom, we should still be sleeping. It's only seven o'clock. We aren't supposed to get up for fifteen more minutes."

Alice's eyebrows shot up. "I *thought* I was still tired," she exclaimed. "Now I know why. But it's too much work to get ready for bed again. What's next?"

"Breakfast."

"We've already done that too! What does she say after that?" She snatched the list from me, and her shoulders slumped. "Oh. Dishes." She slapped the paper back on the table. "But that's at eight, so we shouldn't do them yet. Play a game with me instead."

I groaned. Alice loves games and plays to win, even early in the morning, and I didn't feel awake enough to focus on Mastermind or checkers.

"Sorry, but I think since we're supposed to be sleeping right now we should do something quiet," I said. "It should be something so quiet, we might as well be sleeping. I'm going to go read in bed."

Alice sighed. "OK. I will do that too." She went up the stairs and hopped on her bed with a book. But she really must have been tired because after a few minutes the book fell out of her hands and she started to snore.

Following Mom's directions exactly, I did the dishes at eight. But with Alice sleeping in the bedroom, I couldn't make my bed or tidy up like I was supposed to do at eight-fifteen. I decided to go out in the rowboat instead.

Milo already knows how to row. He learned at Boy Scout camp a few years ago. Alice is utterly determined to learn how and seems to have natural coordination. But I don't, and it's embarrassing when your little sister can row a heavy boat all the way down the canal, and you go in circles or get stuck in the reeds along the side. With Milo on the computer and Alice sleeping, it seemed like a good time to try to improve without witnesses, and I headed down to the dock. I stepped gingerly into the rowboat and untied it.

It's a dinosaur of a rowboat, with peeling red paint and awkward, heavy green oars. I pushed away from the dock, trying not to disturb the thick groups of water lilies by our dock. The canal ends in a sluice only a few yards down, so hardly anyone comes down this far to stir them up.

I tried to remember what Milo's hands do when he rows. He makes them move in a rhythm, and it looks easy when he does it. But I kept veering off into the bank, barely managing to avoid the neighboring dock. Nobody seemed to be around to see me, and I backed out and turned around. The sun broke through the morning fog just then and lit up the canal. It was quiet, with no sounds but water lapping against the boat and the faraway rumble of a tractor. It was so peaceful I let the boat drift.

I was completely alone. There wasn't anyone in the world, I realized, who knew where I was right at this moment. That was frightening and a little bit wonderful at the same time. It felt comfortable and right to be here, like

I belonged. I found myself talking right out loud to God.

"I'm really worried about Mom, God. Please take care of her, on her way to Missouri by herself. And watch over Grandma Sybil. Make her well again."

Suddenly I remembered how I'd yelled at Milo yesterday and even shoved him. I felt guilty.

"Please, God, I don't even know how to stop the stupid fights I keep having with Milo. I need help to stop doing it." I wondered if it would be all right to pray for God to make Milo stop aggravating me instead of teaching me to control myself. It seemed like it would be so much easier to start with Milo, but I decided to leave that off and finish it up.

"It's so beautiful here, God. I wish I could stay forever. I wish I really did belong here. I wish I belonged somewhere."

That thought usually depressed me, but somehow this morning it didn't. I still felt peaceful and happy, and today I couldn't even worry about moving to Oregon, and maybe California or somewhere else a year after that. I started trying to row the boat again and managed to get a few hundred feet farther. But before I could congratulate myself on this achievement, I got turned around with the oars, and I really did smack right into a dock. And this time, someone saw me.

An old man in a crisp-looking plaid bathrobe was sitting in a chair a few yards away, reading the newspaper. He looked over his paper at me, and I waved and smiled, trying to give him the impression that I really knew what I was doing and could get the boat away from his dock with no problem. But I couldn't. I kept going in circles. Out of the corner of my eye I could see him watching me, and his paper lowered inch by inch until I could see a white mustache. I thought it might be twitching.

"I'm sorry," I called, and then remembered I was in a foreign country, and he might not speak English. But he answered back in a perfect British accent.

"Do you need a push to get straightened around, then?"

The reeds along the bank began to shake and I saw the top of Alice's head bobbing my way. "That would be great, thank you," I said, hoping he could hurry and do it fast so Alice wouldn't see me having to be rescued.

But the man wasn't in a hurry. He got up slowly, folding the paper into a perfect rectangle and placing it on the chair. He walked toward me with sort of a lurch, and I could see that his left leg didn't seem to work correctly. I pretended not to notice. He leaned over, grunting a little, and I felt bad that he would have to get up again after he finished helping me. There was certainly nothing wrong with his arms, though. He gave the boat a tremendous push that twirled it in an elegant half-circle. Just as he finished, Alice ran right into his yard.

"Charlotte, it's almost ten," she called, panting. "Mommy's list says you're supposed to be reading to me. I have my books all picked out." I don't think she even noticed my rescuer until then. "Oh, hi," she said uncertainly. But the uncertainty didn't last long. Alice has never met a stranger in her life.

She stuck out her hand, the one that wasn't holding an armful of picture books, and said, "I'm Alice. I'm one of your new neighbors. We live down there for the summer." She flashed a smile, full of little holes where she's waiting for new teeth, and pointed down at our rental house, barely visible through the reeds.

I cringed. Mom and Dad have told us that we shouldn't expect Dutch people to be as friendly as Americans, but I guess Alice forgot, or maybe she just didn't believe them. The man smiled back at her, stuck out his own hand, and said, "It's a pleasure to meet you, Alice. I'm Pieter de Hooch."

"Just like my painting," I gasped, and then I felt like a complete idiot.

Alice's eyes got huge and she stepped back respectfully. "Did you do it?" she demanded. "Are you the famous artist who painted Charlotte's favorite picture in the gallery?"

The man chuckled and shook his head. "No. I'm afraid I'm no relation at all. The artist de Hooch lived hundreds of years ago. I enjoy art, but I'm afraid I can't even draw. My work is in..." He paused. "Communications. Mostly by computer these days."

"My daddy does most of his work on the computer, too," Alice said reassuringly. "It's okay. It's still real work. And you speak English really great." I was afraid she was going to say he sounded like Jeeves and Wooster, but she didn't.

"Thank you," Mr. De Hooch replied. "My wife and I lived in England for several years, and we've visited your own wonderful country many times."

His mustache twitched again, although his leg creaked when he stood up. Both he and I winced. He turned to look at me. "I take it you are the Charlotte who likes the painter. And I also take it that you're new to rowing. I suggest you give the oars more room, and let them dip into the water a bit deeper before you pull back. You'll soon get the hang of it."

"Thanks, Mr. de Hooch," I said. "It was nice to meet you."

"And nice to meet you too," he said. "That house usually has different people renting it every week all summer. I'm glad to hear there will just be one family. I'll be watching for you." With effort, he lowered himself back in the chair and unfolded the newspaper. Before his face disappeared behind it he looked over it at me once more. "Until you get to rowing a little more reliably, please be careful of the statuary on my dock. We were lucky this time."

Before now, I'd been too busy and embarrassed to pay much attention to his dock. Five big bowls of red geraniums lined the side, but in between these were whimsical statues of frogs, a few beavers, and an otter.

"These are awesome," I said. "I'll be careful for sure."

"Have a good day," Mr. De Hooch said. He raised his paper up all the way again and ignored us as Alice skipped over to the dock and handed me her books.

"Let me get in and ride back home with you," she begged. "I haven't been in the boat for so long. Not for a whole day!" She leaped in before I could say yes or no, and then she looked at me expectantly.

What had Mr. De Hooch said? Let the oars out a little more, and let them sink in deeper. I did that. I concentrated on moving both my arms together, and gave it everything I had. The boat turned the wrong direction.

The newspaper didn't move, but Mr. De Hooch called out quietly, "The other way, Charlotte."

Oh. I sunk the oars in deeply, but pulled the opposite direction. Like magic, the boat turned around. I pulled again and again until I could feel a rhythm starting.

"Can I have a turn?" Alice asked hopefully as the dock vanished behind us.

"No," I said. "I'm finally having fun." And I was. I managed to get us back down the canal and only ran the boat into the reeds once.

"I liked that man," Alice said abruptly. "I liked his frogs especially. I wonder if he's named them. Maybe he would let me do it if he hasn't already."

I was concentrating so hard on rowing that for a minute I'd forgotten about the man we'd just met. Unlike Alice, I was more interested in him than his statues. He seemed like the kind of person who'd be more comfortable wearing a suit than sitting next to his dock in a bathrobe, even on a summer morning. And what had happened to his leg? I felt a journal entry coming on. Annabeth would be proud.

5

Provisions

By the time we tied the rowboat to the dock, put the oars away, and read Alice's books, it was lunchtime. There was enough bread and cheese in the tiny refrigerator to feed the three of us, but just barely, and not much else in the kitchen. Since we don't have a car, all our groceries have to fit in the saddlebags of the bikes. You can't get much into them, so we have to go to the store nearly every day. We hadn't gone yesterday because of the trip to Amsterdam.

"I'll ride over to the village after lunch," I said, as Milo stared into the refrigerator, clearly hoping its contents would miraculously multiply.

"No, we'll all go," Milo said. He grinned at me. "I want to make sure you get the right stuff." Get the right chocolate is what he probably meant, but company sounded good to me.

"We should just go now," he said, looking at the lunch dishes piled in the sink. "We'll have plenty of other stuff to put away when we get back anyway. We can clean everything up all at once. It will be more efficient." He got some money from Dad's bedside drawer, and we went out the door, locking it behind us on the way to the bike shed.

A few minutes later, we were bumping down the road to the path across the field. Alice rode on the back of Milo's bike. The house had come with four full-sized bikes, but all of these were too big for Alice. Dad planned to rent one for her, but he hadn't had a chance to do it yet.

In every field we passed, farmers on tractors seemed to be busy bringing in hay. It was a quiet, picture-book scene, until a scream from Alice shattered the peace. Milo slammed on his breaks so quickly I'm surprised both of them didn't sail into the ditch. "What is it?" he demanded. "What's wrong?"

One look at Alice and I knew she was fine. "There!" she said, pointing excitedly. "Just look at them!"

In the middle of a newly-shorn field stood two motionless storks, staring right back at us. I almost expected to see a pink or blue blanket grasped between their beaks and a newborn baby snuggled inside.

"It's like *The Wheel on the School!*" Alice bounced on the back of the bike in delight. Before our trip, Mom had read Alice a story about some Dutch schoolchildren who wanted to bring storks back to their village, Shora.

With quiet dignity, the birds stalked across the field. They were huge—half as tall as Milo, or maybe even Dad.

"Storks come all the way from Africa," Alice informed us, proud of her knowledge. "That's a very long trip for them. Mommy and I looked it up on the map." She turned around on the bike toward me. "Charlotte, can you make me a list of all the animals I've seen since we came here? Put the storks on it. And the frogs and beaver and otter at Mr. de Hooch's. And don't forget those lizards in the park in Amsterdam. They were the best of all. I want to go see them again."

"When we get home," I promised.

We took off down the path again, leaving the storks behind. I could barely hear Alice singing a hymn as she sat behind Milo. It sounded like *His Eye is on the Sparrow*. I guess that was as close to a song about storks as she could think of.

The sun shone, and I was almost too warm in my

sweater. I could hear some of the louder birds and the tractors in the fields as we pedaled along. It was one o'clock. Mom's plane was probably just about to take off at the Amsterdam airport. I didn't want to think about that, so I pedaled faster. I caught up with Milo and passed him. Then he passed me. There were no other riders on this long stretch of the path, and I pedaled harder, trying to catch up with him again. "We're beating you, we're beating you," Alice chanted, and Milo grinned and gained a few more yards. He looked back to give me a thumbs-up.

I saw what was going to happen before he did and yelled a warning right before he hit the rock. Both he and Alice flew off the bike and into the ditch.

Alice rose slowly, whimpering. Her jacket was dirty, but she looked fine, so I ran to Milo, who got up a lot more slowly. His entire right side was covered in dark brown mud, except for the palm of his hand, which oozed blood the minute he flexed it. Alice screamed.

"I don't think it should be bleeding that much," I said, staring at it.

"Yes, well, it is!" Instead of crying when he gets hurt, Milo gets angry. "Haven't you got a tissue or something in your bag? Don't just stand there."

I ran back to the saddlebag of my bike to check. "The only one I've got is dirty," I called back. "You think a leaf or a reed or something might work?"

"That's a stupid idea," Milo said, holding his hand against one of the few clean spots on his jacket. "Like I could keep either of those on while I ride."

His tone of voice made me mad, and instead of being worried about Milo's hand, I just wanted to slug him. But I didn't. Milo snatched off his jacket and wrapped it around his hand, screwing up his face while he did so.

"You'd better go back," I said. "I don't think you can

finish riding into town and you look terrible."

"You think?" Milo said, sarcastically. "It's going to be so much fun trying to get back to the house, riding one-handed." He started limping toward his bike, which was lying wheels up on the path. "You better go on to the store anyway. We need the groceries." His shoulders sagged and he didn't look mad anymore. With his left hand he reached awkwardly into his pants pocket and got the money. He handed it to me without saying a word.

"Do you want me to come back with you to make sure you get there all right?" I asked.

"I'll be fine," Milo said. "It would probably be good if you took Alice with you, though. I don't think I'll be riding very steady, and she might not be safe on the back of my bike." He hobbled to his bike and picked it up. Alice and I watched while he got on and rode back in the direction of the house. At first the bike wobbled all over the path, but in a minute it straightened out and I knew he'd probably make it back to the house.

"Come on, Alice," I said. "Let's get this done fast so we can get back to Milo."

She hopped on behind me. I haven't ridden with her before, and I thought she might be heavy on the back of my bike, but it wasn't too bad. Alice wrapped her arms around my waist, and almost before we started going she was humming again. We passed more farms, and Alice waved to the ponies grazing in the field before we got to town.

At the traffic circle outside the village, I slowed way down. I didn't want to take a chance on having an accident myself. I'd come to the grocery store a few times with Mom or Dad, but never alone before, and I was nervous I wouldn't find it. I took a wrong turn, but by looking for the church steeples, I found the business section of town.

As we slowly passed the bakery, we saw the baker's assistant take unsold loaves out of window displays and close the curtains. We passed the hardware store, a jewelry shop, the drugstore, and a coffee house before we coasted to a stop outside Smit's, the grocery store. "The family business," Dad joked, the first time we went there. "We ought to ask for a discount."

"Have you ever done the shopping without Mom before?" Alice asked as we dismounted, and I shook my head.

"I haven't even picked out dinner by myself before. This is going to be fun. What do we need again?"

"We used up the milk," Alice said. "And we're out of chocolate. That's the main thing." She looked as excited as I felt. "Can we have noodles for supper? I like noodles."

"Noodles are easy," I agreed. We went over to the pasta section and I picked up a box of spaghetti. "What do we want on top?" I asked. "How about spaghetti sauce? That's easy, too."

The spaghetti sauce came in boxes instead of jars, and of course I couldn't read the writing to know exactly what we were choosing, but we picked one with a tasty-looking picture and put it in the cart. "Mom would want us to have a vegetable," I said.

"Isn't tomato sauce a vegetable?" Alice asked. "Tomatoes grow in Grandma Sybil's garden."

"Close enough," I agreed. "I don't know how to cook vegetables anyway. I barely know noodles."

Mom likes to cook, and sometimes she laments that she's failed in teaching this skill to Milo and me. Every now and then she'll make us help in the kitchen for a few meals. Then she forgets all about it and goes back to doing everything herself, humming to music or watching TV. She likes her quiet time too much to conduct cooking lessons for very long.

"What else do we need?" Alice asked. "Aren't we out of cereal?"

"Yes. At least I won't have to cook that," I said. We chose cereal with big apple chunks in it, and then went around the corner to the candy aisle. We thought that after Milo's accident and Mom's departure, tonight's chocolate bar ought to be a big one, with more squares available to divide. We could all use some cheering up.

I knew we should probably hurry home to Milo, but I kept putting off the final moment when I would have to check out at the register. The last time we came, we got a friendly cashier who spoke great English because she'd been a foreign exchange student in Iowa. But the first time, the girl didn't really speak English at all, and it was embarrassing as she pantomimed that we needed to bag the groceries that had piled up at the end of the counter. We hadn't known to bring along grocery bags, so we carried all the loose groceries in our arms out of the store. It was a good thing all five of us went shopping that day or we couldn't have carried it all. We stuffed them in our saddle bags and then went straight to the household store to purchase reusable bags.

Those bags, I realized, were still hanging up on the coat hooks in the hall at home. Milo and I had forgotten all about them in our hurry to get to the store, but it didn't really matter. We only had a few things. I sighed with relief when I saw that the friendly Iowa girl was working again today, and I chose her line, even though it was longer. Just knowing I could talk to her if I needed to made me relax.

"Shopping for your mom?" she asked with a friendly smile.

I could see Alice gearing up for a long explanation of Mom's departure, which would probably include our entire family history starting back who knows when, possibly with the Smit family's emigration to America a hundred years ago, so I cut her off before she could get started. "Yes," I said. "It's the first time we've been here alone. Thanks." Alice scowled at me as she helped gather up the groceries, but by the time we got to the rack of fresh flowers near the door, she'd forgiven me. We stopped to admire the roses and daisies.

"We should have bought some of these," Alice said, burying her nose in one of the lower bouquets. "They don't even cost much money."

"They'd look great in our front window," I agreed.

We stuffed our groceries inside my bike's saddle bag, and I unlocked the bike and got on. Alice hopped on behind me and we set off down the main street. We'd no sooner got started when I hit the brake. "Wait a minute. Do we have a first aid kit at the house to take care of Milo's hand?"

"We've got band-aids," Alice informed me. "I saw Mom unpack them."

"He needs more than Band-Aids," I said. We parked the bike and went into the drugstore to buy bigger bandages and some tape.

A few minutes later, Alice and I were back on the long open stretch toward the rental house. I rode carefully, mindful of Milo and the rock. But it was smooth sailing all the way home.

When we got to the house, we found Milo lying down on his bed. He'd washed up a little and changed into clean clothes, but he was holding a towel against his hand. "Hasn't it stopped bleeding yet?" I asked, surprised.

Milo shrugged. "It was still kind of oozing about fifteen minutes ago. I haven't checked since then."

I felt bad that he'd had to come back to the empty

house and fix himself up. He was missing Mom, too, and probably a lot right now, although he would never say so. I showed him the bandages and the tape, and he cheered up a little. Alice showed him the chocolate bar, and he cheered up even more.

I cringed when he took the towel off his hand. The towel looked nasty, caked with blood and dirt, and Alice pinched one hand over her nose as she carried the towel to the laundry room. I wondered how to get bloodstains out of towels. I hoped Dad knew because for sure I didn't.

Fortunately, Milo's hand wasn't bleeding anymore, and he was able to clean it himself at the kitchen sink. I rummaged through some of the things Mom had left behind and found packets of antibacterial ointment, which I squeezed onto Milo's hand before we put on the new bandage. We had to use a lot of tape to get it to stay on, but the whole thing was good and tight when we finished, and it looked impressively large.

"Can't we eat dinner now?" Alice asked plaintively. "I'm hungry from riding to the village and from all the fresh air."

"It's only four o'clock," I protested. "So no, it's way too early for dinner. I think we eat at six, and we should wait for Dad anyway."

Alice hurried to the table to check Mom's schedule, our definitive guide. She sighed loudly. "She says we're supposed to be outside right now, getting more fresh air."

"Well, I don't know about you, but I've had all the fresh air I can stand for one day," Milo said. He went to the desk in the dining area and sat down at Dad's laptop. He tried to play a game, but couldn't use his right hand. "Left handed, I'm terrible," he mumbled. "This is not going to work." He started a new game but his score was lower than Alice's would have been, and his character died in about thirty seconds.

"What can you do now, Milo?" Alice asked. "Because with only one hand, you can't really ride your bike. You can't row the boat. You can't play darts, and you can't play on the computer." She consulted Mom's list again. "You can't even vacuum or sweep or any of these things you're supposed to do."

"Thanks, I feel even better now," Milo said. "Some of that stuff I hadn't even thought about."

"You can read," I said brightly. "And watch TV."

"We only get Dutch channels," Milo said. "And I hardly brought any books with me. That was stupid."

"Mom brought plenty," I reminded him, but he rolled his eyes.

"It's OK, you can read mine!" Alice jumped up and ran for the small pile of books she'd packed in her carry on. "You can read them aloud to me. It says for Charlotte to do it on the schedule, but we can put you down instead. Read to me now. Read to me about Frances the badger and how she would only eat bread and jam. That one's my favorite."

We've all read Frances so many times we have the book nearly memorized, and I thought for sure Milo would outright refuse this request. He didn't, so he really must have been bored. Unfortunately, after a few pages he started adding words to the story, making Frances speak in a Martian voice.

"No!" Alice cried, looking in horror at Milo. "You can't do that to Frances. She doesn't talk like that. Her mother wouldn't let her."

I knew how the session would end even before Milo switched to a squeaky mouse voice, adding in a paragraph about Frances stockpiling machine guns in her closet and making plans to rob the local bank. Alice grabbed her book protectively, jumped off the couch, and ran to hide it in her room.

"Well, that was good for about five minutes," I said to him. "What are you going to do now?"

Milo didn't bother answering but went outside, and I could see him wandering around the yard, sort of aimlessly. Alice came downstairs, holding her life jacket. "I'm going out to practice rowing," she said. Dad allows her on the rowboat as long as the guide rope is still tied to the dock. She never gets very far but it keeps her busy forever.

Milo took off down the road for a walk. After having and losing the ability to go almost anywhere fast on a bike, being on foot probably felt like walking backwards to him. I decided to start getting supper ready.

Just as I got the water boiling for noodles, Dad walked in. Still wearing her life jacket, Alice came in from the boat and ran over to give him a hug.

"Miss Alice!" Dad said. "I'm so relieved to see you alive. I think Mom was afraid one of you would need stitches before I could get home to take you to the hospital."

This felt a little too close to the truth. "Milo got wounded on our way to the store," Alice told him. "Not just a little wounded, either. It bled and bled and bled and he had to come home. Do you want to see the towel that mopped up all the blood? And his jacket, from before that?"

Dad's eyes took in the living area in one quick sweep. "Where is he?" he demanded. "Where is Milo?" I think he envisioned Milo lying in a corner somewhere in a pool of blood, unconscious.

"He's fine, Dad, really," I said. "He fell off his bike and cut himself pretty bad across the hand, but the bleeding stopped and we've got it all bandaged up. He can't really row or bike or anything, so he went for a walk."

"Well, I'm relieved to hear he's OK," Dad said. But he didn't sound relieved. Mom is the one who always worries, while Dad thinks nothing bad will ever happen. I don't think it made him feel very good that within hours of him taking charge of us, a lot of blood did happen.

"Let's not mention this to Mom if we can avoid it," he said. "Once she gets to Missouri, she'll have plenty to worry about with Grandma Sybil."

"If we Skype, she will see the bandage," Alice informed him. "It's so big it looks like a cast."

The water on the stove started to boil over, and I ran to turn it down and then dumped in the noodles. I put another pan on the stove and cut open the sealed plastic box the sauce came in.

"Spaghetti is a good idea," Dad said approvingly. "Quick and simple. We're going to have to make a list of meals like that for while we're on our own, if your mother hasn't already done it for us." He bent over to open the fridge and looked around in it like Milo had, clearly disappointed by the small amount of food inside. He made a snack of the last piece of cheese and a few leftover crackers.

Alice set the table. She looked out the window and called to Dad, "Milo's coming down the road. Look, you can see his bandage all the way from here!" Dad looked up from the computer and out the window at Milo.

"Hmmmm," he said, and he didn't sound happy. When Milo came in, Dad had him take the bandage off so he could examine the cut. "I think we'd better wash that again," he said. "Alice, get the bag of first aid stuff from the suitcase. We need more ointment, too."

Dad's good at blood and injuries, and when he was done, Milo's bandage looked a lot more professional. Dad even added some extra padding to the palm of Milo's hand. "You're probably fine to bike on it, son, but you'd better leave the boats alone for a while. Too much pressure. It might rip it right back open. Give it a few days to heal."

I knew Milo had to be disappointed about the boats, but selfishly I wasn't. It would give me more time to practice with the rowboat and get better at it.

The noodles stuck to the pan but once they were in a serving bowl nobody would notice. I brought bread and butter to the table and we all sat down. We joined hands, except Alice who held Milo's elbow instead of his bandage, and Dad gave the blessing.

I was just pouring the sauce on my noodles when Dad made a strangled sound, bolted out of his chair, and ran for the sink.

"What's the matter, Daddy?" Alice asked, but Dad couldn't reply. He rinsed his mouth with water, then spit it all back into the sink, nearly choking on the second glass he tossed down. He spit the water out when he saw me start to put a bite of spaghetti in my mouth.

"Don't eat it," he shouted, and I dropped the fork on my plate, staring at him. How could my cooking be that bad?

He gave his mouth another rinse. "It's not the kind of spaghetti sauce we're used to," he said. The words came in a wheeze. "Sorry Charlotte. The Dutch used to own Indonesia and many people here eat spicy Indonesian food. That sauce has some of the hottest peppers I think I've ever tasted in my life. Wow." He filled his glass from the faucet and grabbed a paper towel. There were tears coming out of his eyes.

"Dad, I'm so sorry," I said. I felt terrible.

"There's no way you could possibly have known," Dad said. "I'm sure the spiciness of those things was written across the package somewhere, but since you don't read Dutch, you missed it. It could have happened to anyone, including me or Mom." His smile was a little forced and his eyes kept watering. "Don't feel bad about it."

"But we don't have anything else to eat," Milo pointed out, looking at our plates. All of us already had sauce spread over our noodles, and we'd used all the pasta in the box. "I mean, really, we don't," Milo said. "There's nothing else to eat. Except breakfast cereal. And our bread and butter."

"Then we'll have that." Dad opened the cupboard and took out the cereal, and then leaned down to the fridge to get the milk. He closed the door to the fridge slowly and he didn't have to tell us the bad news. Alice and I had forgotten to buy milk and there was none left from this morning.

I was already on my feet. "We'll ride to the store right now, get the milk, and buy something else for dinner."

Milo pointed to the clock. "The store closes in ten minutes," he said. "And it takes twenty minutes to ride into town."

"And it's closed all day tomorrow. Sunday," I said slowly. I'd completely forgotten about that. Apparently, we all had.

It's strange how much hungrier you feel the minute you know you might not have a solid meal for thirty-six hours until the stores open again. Ossenzijl doesn't have fast food. The only restaurants open on Sunday are fancy little places with expensive menus that would blow our grocery budget for the entire week if we ate there one time. So I knew we'd be scrounging for whatever we could. It only took Dad, Milo, and Alice about ten seconds to reach the same conclusion before we were all in the kitchen, pulling what little food we had onto the counter.

"There's the giant chocolate bar," Alice said, waving it. "It's so big it's almost like a whole dinner."

"And we'll enjoy it too," Dad assured her. "Put it over there."

"There's the rolls we almost ate tonight, plus butter," I said. "They're still on the table."

"Bring the plate to the counter," Dad told me. "I need to get a visual on everything."

He rummaged through the drawers and produced a container of coffee, an unopened jar of hazelnut spread, about a quart of dried oats, a jar of peanut butter, some ancient blocks of what looked like some kind of soup broth starter, and about half a cup of sugar.

"All that's left in the fridge are two containers of yogurt and more butter," Milo said.

Alice ran up the stairs and came down a minute later. "I saved my peanuts from the plane," she cried proudly. She put the tiny packet on the counter.

"Every little bit helps," Dad said, but he didn't sound convinced. We stood and stared at the little pile of food that would need to keep us nourished until Monday.

"I think we should wash the noodles," Milo said. "Get the hot sauce off them and maybe boil them a little bit again, and then eat them. Plain. It's something, anyway."

"I agree," Dad said. "At least it would be filling." He snapped his fingers. "Alice, you gave me an idea with the peanuts. Let's check all the suitcases, and look through everything we brought along. Maybe we have more food than we think. Didn't Mom bring some emergency stuff? It seems like she did. I hope we haven't eaten that already." He hurried off to his bedroom and we scattered to check through our own things.

A minute later, there was a triumphant shout. Dad came out of his bedroom, waving some pancake mix, a few pouches of tuna, and a handful of Mom's favorite protein bars. I ran back with some packaged cookies from dinner on the plane. Milo had a bag of dried beans.

"Mom must have put them in the pocket of my suitcase," he said. "I didn't even know they were there."

We dumped everything we'd found on the counter, and we all felt relieved because the pile looked a lot more significant than it had before.

"We'll start soaking these beans right away," Dad said. "Maybe we can add the tuna and make a kind of soup. That'll be dinner tomorrow." We groaned, but Dad was grinning now. "Come on kids, where's the Smith pioneer spirit? These may not be tasty meals, necessarily, but we won't starve. We can have the pancakes for breakfast and put yogurt on top. We can each have a protein bar for lunch, maybe with the rolls we were going to eat tonight. We can spread them with the hazelnut spread. We'll go to the store early on Monday, before breakfast. We're going to be fine. Let's give these noodles a bath."

We washed the sauce off the noodles and heated them back up again. Then we returned them to our plates.

"Just plain noodles don't taste very good," Alice said, staring at them unhappily. "I wish we had something on top. Spaghetti sauce or even barbecue sauce, like the kind Uncle Jack makes."

Dad reached around, picked up the jar of hazelnut chocolate spread and a spoon, and gave them to Alice. "Here. Jazz them up a little."

"Chocolate spaghetti?" Alice sounded horrified but looked delighted. She dug her spoon into the gooey spread in the jar and twirled her noodles around in it. She took a bite. "Oooooooh, it's good!" she cried. "You guys should try it."

Milo didn't have to be asked twice, and then we

passed the jar around, careful to leave enough to eat with our bread tomorrow. "Butter would make it even better," he said, and we each added a chunk of that too, watching it melt over the chocolate and then mixing it up. It was a tantalizing sight.

"We could sell this," Milo said, stuffing his mouth with more. "Why don't more people make pasta into a dessert? It totally works. We should do it again."

"Well, hopefully, if we do it will be a choice rather than a necessity," Dad said. "We're going to need to plan to stay on top of the groceries a little better, especially on the weekends. But it's just one of those things we have to learn. Fortunately, it's only a minor inconvenience tonight." He took another bite of chocolate spaghetti and gave a smile of contentment. Then his eye fell on Mom's schedule on the other side of the table and he picked it up, reading through it for the first time.

"Just curious, kids. How closely did you stick to this today?"

Silence. "Minimally," I finally confessed. "But we did look at it a few times."

"Well, tomorrow's another start," Dad said. "It's Sunday, and I want us all to go to church in the village. Maybe we can bring along the protein bars and have a little picnic somewhere afterwards if the weather is nice. But I want all of you to do what Mom's list says. That way, if there are any more accidents with injuries, or any emergencies with food, I can at least tell her we were trying."

He looked around the room. "And besides, we want the owners to be happy with what they find when we give them back the key to this house. So the housekeeping chores are mandatory. And that goes for you, too," he said, looking Milo right in the eye. "Mom's got you on cooking rotation and cleaning along with Charlotte. And I don't want to see you trying to shunt any of it off on your sister unless you really can't do it due to your hand. Got it?"

"Yes, sir," Milo said. He was enjoying the chocolate spaghetti so much he barely looked up.

It would be fun to be the lady of this house, I thought. Our picture window already looked a little spotty, and suddenly I wanted it to be just as clean as the others up and down the road. I should bring some flowers in for the table. Maybe I could dust, and then rearrange the knick-knacks above the fireplace. Dad was right. Tomorrow was a new start, and tomorrow we would do it right.

6

Making Good

Mom's list said to get up at seven-fifteen, so seven-fifteen it would be. I jumped out of bed the minute the alarm went off. Alice, on the other side of the bed, didn't even flinch, which was just fine with me. I was glad to have the morning to myself. Mom knew I liked getting up early, so she'd assigned breakfast to me. I went downstairs to the kitchen to find the pancake mix we'd brought along from Boston.

After last night's spaghetti sauce debacle, it reassured me to be able to read the directions in English, right on the pancake package. Cooking in English was easy and fun compared to cooking in Dutch.

The tile floor felt cold on my feet. I shivered a little and went to the hall to get my shoes. I could hear Milo moving around up in his room upstairs, and the shower running in the bathroom. That must be Dad. I glanced up at the clock. Mom had probably landed in Missouri several hours ago. I hoped she was sleeping now, like Alice. I put the frying pan on the stovetop and turned on the burner.

While I waited for it to heat up, I looked out the window toward the canal, through the little bit of mist the sun hadn't burned away yet. The rowboat bobbed gently on the water. This afternoon I'd try rowing again. I'd go down and see if Mr. de Hooch sits out every day or just on Saturday mornings. And what about his wife? Was there still a Mrs. de Hooch? I thought back to the few things he'd said to us and realized I couldn't be sure. Maybe that was why he limped. Maybe there'd been a terrible accident. They'd been biking together, and then a car—

The frying pan started to smoke and I grabbed it off the stove for a minute so it could cool off. I put it back on the burner and focused on making pancakes. During one of my few cooking lessons with Mom, she'd taught me how to make sure pancakes turned out brown instead of white or black. Get the skillet hot enough. Don't turn them too early. Don't turn them too late. I remembered what she said, and they came out just right.

"Good work, Charlotte," Dad said during breakfast later. "These hit the spot, even without maple syrup."

"I wonder how they'd be with hazelnut spread," Milo said meditatively.

"Let's try it!" Alice had been eating slowly, still only half awake, but the mention of hazelnut spread woke her up fast and her eyes sparkled.

"No!" I said. "We're saving that for lunch, like Dad said last night."

"I think we need to stock up on that spread tomorrow," Milo said firmly. "It's magic sauce, I'm telling you. It improves everything. Without Mom here to cook, lots of meals will need improvement."

"Hey!" I protested. "Dad said what happened with the hot peppers could even have happened to Mom!"

"OK, OK," Milo said. "I didn't mean to get you riled up. I'm on the cooking schedule too, so it could be mine that will need help. I'm just saying that the stuff is amazing. I don't understand why we don't have it in America."

"We do," Dad replied. "Only it's called Nutella and it's an expensive treat for a family with three children who would probably inhale it in a day, so we don't buy it. I don't know why it's so cheap here. It's less than a fourth of the

American price. And it tastes even better. Magic sauce. I like that, Milo."

The jar was still on the kitchen counter, and we all stared at it with weakening willpower. "Just on one little pancake?" Alice wheedled. "I will eat my roll with only butter later. Or even eat it dry."

"I guess it doesn't matter when we eat it," Dad said, folding. "Go ahead and dig in." We did. It put all of us in a good mood right away.

"How's your hand today?" I asked Milo.

"It hurt like crazy trying to get to sleep," he admitted. "But it doesn't hurt this morning."

"Good," Dad said. He looked at us all sternly. "You are, all three of you, forbidden to hurt yourselves again, in any way, for the remainder of the summer. No broken bones. No wounds. A few bruises from falling off the bikes are permissible, but that's it, and keep this in mind as you plan your activities." We laughed as we finished our breakfast.

Dad did the dishes, and Alice helped. I went upstairs to get ready for church. Our church back in Boston is casual, and we usually just wear our everyday clothes. But Mom told me to bring a skirt along in case people dressed up more here, and I thought it might be best to wear it this first time. I found a dress for Alice, too, and laid it out on her bed.

I had a detailed Alice list from Mom. "Dad and Milo are not going to notice these things, Charlotte, so I'm counting on you," she'd written. "Make sure she wears clean clothes and that they match. Check her hair and face every time she leaves the house. Bath every other day at least and right away if she falls into the canal like I'm afraid she's going to. I don't want her to look like she's motherless." I wouldn't let Mom down. Alice looked more than presentable after I'd done her hair and got her dressed up.

Dad and Milo took off on their bikes, Dad with Alice behind him. But I realized quickly that riding in a skirt was going to be a challenge. It blew up while I pedaled. I had to stop several times to tuck it down but it kept working its way out. Was there a secret to it? Hopefully I would figure it out fast and not disgrace myself in the process.

"Why are we going to church, again?" Milo called to Dad on the path. "They won't speak English there, so it's not like we're going to get anything out of it."

"The Smith family goes to church on Sunday," Dad called back. "And I very much disagree that you won't get anything out of it, even if you don't understand it."

Once we got to town, we joined many other people on bikes, all pedaling toward one of the three churches. Two were the big ones with spires that had guided me into town yesterday. One of these was a Catholic church, Dad told us, and the other a Protestant Reformed church. We'd go to the Protestant church, and maybe another week try the tiny chapel, also Protestant, near the grocery store.

The churchyard was crowded with bikes of all sizes. We found a place to park ours and locked them. I put my key in the pocket of my bag very carefully so as not to lose it. Without unlocking the bike, the wheels wouldn't turn, and I certainly didn't want to have to walk four miles home.

The building was so full it was hard to find four seats together, and Alice and I had to share a tall, uncomfortable ladder-backed chair. It didn't look like our worship center in Boston at all. This church was built like a mini-cathedral. Its stone walls had wooden arches over the top, and the checkerboard marble floor looked a lot like the one in my painting at the Rijksmuseum.

Unlike church at home, where everyone talks, and

hugs, and drinks coffee while waiting for the service to start, here there was only a quiet hum of whispered conversations until the enormous back door banged shut for the final time, and the pastor and some other men walked down the aisle. As they did this, the congregation went dead silent. It was so quiet you could hear footsteps echoing all the way to the front. The stairs creaked as the pastor climbed the pulpit, which was elevated above the congregation to one side like a giant, elaborately carved wooden mushroom.

A pipe organ began to play, and Dad handed us each hymnals he'd picked up on the way in, pointing to a board where the numbers were listed. We scrambled to find the first one.

At home, we can barely hear the congregation singing above the band in front, but not here. The voices of the congregation surged over the organ, and it was like nothing I've ever heard in church before. The congregation sang in parts, and it was so beautiful it almost didn't seem real. Their voices filled the whole sanctuary.

Even though they were singing in Dutch, I tried to follow along and sing with them. It wasn't that hard to do, since the last words in a line always rhymed. Every now and then I would see a word I knew, or one that sounded like an English word. I was proud of myself that without speaking Dutch, I could piece together part of what the hymn was saying. Amen, Father. Jesus Christ, your Word. I didn't need to know what everything meant. I knew then why Dad had brought us, and I was glad, even though Milo was right that I didn't get anything out of the sermon at all and that it seemed to last a really long time.

When the service ended, a few people looked over at us curiously, but nobody said anything or spoke to us. Dad seemed in no hurry to leave. He was listening to the organist playing something complicated that sounded like a musical math puzzle. "It's a Bach fugue, kids," Dad said. "And this is exactly the setting Bach wanted his work to be played." The organ finally started to wind down and Dad got up with a sigh. "Beautiful. Just beautiful. Let's go."

The churchyard was full of laughter and conversations as people unlocked their bikes and left. "Did you pick those protein bars up like I asked you to, Milo?" Dad asked, and Milo nodded. "I was going to suggest we bike the other direction and take a look around, but I noticed you were having a little trouble with that skirt earlier, Charlotte. Maybe we should go home. I told Mom we'd try to Skype her this afternoon anyway."

"Oh, but I wanted a picnic!" Alice said, disappointed.

"Why don't we just eat here?" Milo asked, pointing to the stone benches across from the churchyard. The benches caught the noon sunlight, and it looked like an invitingly warm spot after the chilly building we'd just left. We wheeled our bikes across the road and sat down.

"That was a long time to sit still in there," Alice said as she unwrapped her protein bar and began to eat.

"The chairs were torture," Milo agreed. "But I know you liked the singing, Dad, and it really was amazing."

The churchyard was empty now, and a man locked the front door of the church, pocketed the key, and walked around the corner to the main street. Alice finished her snack lunch and skipped over to a trashcan by the cemetery to throw away her wrapper. She tried the cemetery gate and it swung open.

"Can I go in, Daddy?" she called back.

"Only if you're quiet and respectful," Dad answered. "It's not a playground."

Alice went in, almost on tiptoe, and we all joined her, silently walking along a scuffed dirt path between the graves. It seemed like the same dozen last names just kept repeating from stone to stone. Tuinstra. Huisman. De Vries. Van der Hoff. Ballast. Some of the stones were so ancient and worn down you couldn't read the writing anymore. But one grave was so fresh that the grass was just beginning to grow again after being turned over. I wondered what it must be like to live in one place so long that you could be buried right across from your great-great-grandmother.

On the way home I did a better job keeping track of my skirt, but still it was a relief to change back into jeans. Just as I finished, Dad hollered up the stairs to me that Mom was on Skype, and I ran down, kind of sideways, because the stairs are very steep. Milo and Alice were already talking. I noticed that Milo kept his bandaged arm behind his back.

"Charlotte!" Mom said, after I squeezed in next to Alice so she could see me on screen. "Well, that's everyone, and you're all alive and well."

"I was riding on the back of Milo's bike to the store yesterday, and--" Alice began. I gave her a warning thump on the back and she shot me an angry look.

"What was that for?" Mom asked, because of course she'd seen the whole thing. "I hope you girls aren't quarreling. Can't we have a pleasant talk instead? What did you want to tell me, Alice?"

"I think Charlotte didn't want Alice to mention the stuff that didn't come home from the store," Milo interjected, saving the day. "We forgot about it being closed on Sunday, and our meals will be a little interesting until Monday, but we have plenty to eat. We found the beans and the pancake mix. We even had a picnic today with your protein bars."

"Right outside a graveyard!" Alice said,

enthusiastically.

"How's Grandma Sybil?" I asked, figuring it might be better to change the subject completely.

"She's still annoyed with me for coming," Mom said. "At least, that's what her mouth says, but I really think she's glad I'm here. Goodness though, I don't have enough clothes along for a Missouri summer. I won't be wearing sweaters and long sleeved shirts here for sure." She looked flushed, and fanned herself as she talked to us. I'm not even sure she was aware she was doing it. It's just sort of an automatic response to being at Grandma Sybil's anytime it's not winter.

"OK, kids," Dad said. "Say goodbye to Mom. I want some time alone with my wife."

We all giggled, even Mom and Dad, and said goodbye. Alice, Milo, and I drifted out to the yard.

"I get the boat!" Alice made a run for the rowboat, but then remembered her life jacket and had to run back toward the house, so I made it to the rowboat before she did. Milo stepped in and sat down on the seat behind me.

"Hey!" I said. "What are you doing here?"

"I may not be able to row, but I don't see why I can't ride," Milo said. "Can't I come along, wherever you're going? We probably better wait for the kid, though."

I wasn't confident enough in my rowing yet that I wanted to take Milo along to backseat drive in the boat with me. But I really didn't want Dad to have to leave the house—and Mom—to break up a fight, so I didn't say anything.

The back door banged shut and Alice ran toward the dock, her lifejacket already over her head. "No fair!" she cried. "You two will always get to the boat first because you don't have to wear life jackets."

"Alice, just climb in," I said. "I'll start rowing and you

64

can help later."

I managed to get us going in the right direction. It drove Milo crazy to be watching rather than rowing. I know he really was trying not to criticize because he would stop himself in the middle of sentences whenever I veered off course, so I gritted my teeth and ignored him.

We passed the house next door, which had a plain dock like ours. I think it must be a rental house too, but it seemed to be empty. The house after that had a few garden gnomes and lots of flowering hydrangeas, and I could see a light on inside. We rowed a little farther and reached Mr. de Hooch's dock. I hadn't thought to look at the house yesterday, but now that I could row without concentrating on it every second, I wanted to see what it looked like.

Mr. de Hooch wasn't outside today, which meant I could be as curious as I wanted to without feeling guilty for staring. His yard was huge. I hadn't noticed the size of that yesterday, either. With its neatly mown stripes, the lawn looked like a flawless piece of corduroy. And no wonder I hadn't noticed the house before. All I could see of the house from here was part of a slate roof above a tall fence.

"Is that lady Mr. de Hooch's wife?" Alice asked quietly.

"Who? Where?" I asked, startled. I hadn't seen anyone.

"Over there," Alice whispered. "By the roses. She is just amazing at roses, don't you think? We should ask her for tips. The ones down by our house don't look so good."

A shower of hundreds—no, thousands—of roses in all shades of yellow and gold and white spilled out from the fence. The lady was kneeling down along the corner of the fence, pruning shears in hand. She gathered up the roses she'd just clipped and tossed them into the wheelbarrow behind her and turned around. I stopped staring immediately, trying to look very busy with the oars. In front of me, Alice leaned over the boat in the opposite direction and trailed her hand in the water, as though she hadn't just been pointing to the fence.

Out of the corner of my eye I saw the lady go right back to her work. If she'd noticed us, she paid no attention. I rowed around a bend in the canal and came to another, larger dock with a wooden sailboat moored to it. This must belong to them too because there wasn't another house in sight.

"Yes, I think she has to be his wife," I told Alice when I knew we were safely out of earshot. "They match together, like a lot of married people do. Even working in the garden, she looks sort of elegant."

"She's beautiful," Alice said. "Beautiful in an old-lady kind of way."

"In a rich kind of way," Milo said. "That is an expensive sailboat." The wooden hull of the boat was trimmed with navy blue paint, and its polished brass trim gleamed. "I sure wish I could ride in that," he said, pure envy in his voice. "It's like something out of a magazine."

I liked the boat well enough, but I love roses, and I couldn't get over the fact that the lady (I could only think of her using that word) was going to throw them all away. An entire wheelbarrow full!

"I wish I could have some of her roses," I said. "They'd just make our front window."

Rowing is heavy work even when you're alone, but the extra weight of Milo and Alice really tired me out. I dug the oar in hard and turned around to go home.

"You can sit here and help me row now, Alice," I said.

"I wish I could do it by myself," Alice grumbled. I let her try for about ten seconds, but that was all it took for her to realize she couldn't manage it with all of us in there. It took us a few clumsy minutes to figure out how to work together, and the oars splashed up loudly, getting us wet. Alice squealed and I laughed too as we rounded the corner again, and this time the lady looked up quickly. She frowned and immediately got up and slipped around through the gate and disappeared.

"What's up with that?" Milo asked, puzzled. "Can't we make a little noise? I thought you said the guy was nice to you."

"He was," Alice and I said together.

"Well, his wife doesn't seem to be," Milo said.

"Let's go a little faster away from here, Alice," I said. The sun disappeared behind the clouds, and suddenly the whole world felt a little less friendly than it had just a few minutes before. I felt the first plunk of raindrops before I even saw them.

"Maybe she knew it was going to rain, and that's why she went in," suggested Alice.

"No," Milo said positively. "I saw her face. She went in because of us. I know she did."

The few drops became a steady pattern, and in a remarkably short period of time rain poured down. It hit the canal with so much force that the drops bounced on the surface of the water. Alice and I rowed as hard as we could but we weren't very fast together, and by the time we reached our dock and Milo jumped out to secure the boat, we were almost as drenched as if we'd fallen into the canal. Dad held the back door open as we raced across the yard to shelter.

"Stop!" he ordered, the second we crossed the threshold. We froze. "Shoes and socks off. Jackets off, right here. I'll get some towels."

We slithered out of our things, and once our feet were

dry enough from the towels not to leave tracks all across the floor, we hurried to our rooms to change into dry clothes. I smelled bean soup cooking on the stove downstairs and found myself looking forward to supper. Something hot to warm me up all the way through sounded very appealing, no matter how strange it might taste once Dad got done with it. And there was the chocolate bar for afterwards. That was definitely something to look forward to.

But dinner was still a couple hours away. I flopped on my bed with Annabeth's journal. I had some catching up to do. I sketched pictures of the bike path, the church, and as much as I could remember of Mr. de Hooch's dock. In the square next to that picture, I started to write.

"Dear Journal,

We have a mysterious neighbor. Either that or she really just hates kids. She seemed to dislike us on sight, and I think the feeling is mutual."

7

Rain and Wind

Hard, drumming rain continued all afternoon, and I could still hear it when I woke up during the night. The sun didn't come out the next morning as it had every other day, and I overslept. I got up when I heard a banging sound outside. The sky was dark, and the tree branches along the canal swayed in the wind. It only took one sweep of the yard to locate the source of the noise. In our hurry to get out of the rain yesterday afternoon we'd forgotten to tie both ends of the rowboat to the dock. As the current pulled the boat away, it swung out into the canal before returning to hit the dock with a thump.

I went downstairs. Dad and Milo were already up, bandages and tape spread across the kitchen table. "I'm going to really tape this up well," Dad said to Milo. "I don't want you to have trouble with it on the bike. Judging by how fast the blades on the windmill in town are spinning, we're going to have trouble enough just biking into town."

"It's not raining hard anymore, at least," I said.

"Well, I'm glad about that," Dad said, "but I have a feeling it's still going to be rough ride." He carefully cut the tape on Milo's bandage. "All right, son, let's go get our girls some breakfast." He and Milo put on their jackets.

"Charlotte, if you and Alice get too hungry waiting for us, you can always cook up the oats," Dad reminded me on the way out. "They won't taste as good without milk, but we do still have a little sugar. Or you could eat that apple cereal dry. There's a little bit of Magic Sauce left too, and you may as well finish it up. More will be coming home with us." He winked at me as he and Milo left. The wind slammed the door before they could close it behind them.

Through the window I watched the two of them riding down the bike path through the field. They had just disappeared from view when the sky turned an angrier gray and the storm returned. There was no gentle start, and a violent rain began immediately. I felt sorry for Dad and Milo. I bet Dad hadn't counted on days like today when he and Mom decided we wouldn't need a car to live out here this summer.

I heard the boat crack against the dock again, and knew I'd better fix it. I put on my jacket and shoes and went outside, taking care not to let go of the door until I could close it myself.

Wind and sideways rain hit me so hard it blew my hair across my face and I could barely see. I wished I had taken the time to braid it. I ran to the dock with my hand up in front of my eyes, pushing my hair out of the way. No, this definitely didn't feel like a gentle summer-in-Boston kind of rain. It was a serious, howling rain, and the fact that the temperature wasn't too cold didn't stop me from wishing I had a fire in the fireplace to return to.

The boat was out in the canal when I got there, and I waited a minute until the crash of the next wave smacked it back against the dock. I leaned over, just managing to grab the end of the boat, and slipped the rope through the metal ring. I tied it down as tight as I could and ran back indoors.

I found Alice curled up in a blanket on the couch when I got back inside. "I was scared," she said, looking at me disapprovingly. "I came downstairs and everyone was gone. I thought you'd all gone away and left me." I sat down beside her and she wrapped the blanket around us both. "Remember the part in *Little House on the Prairie*, where Pa goes off to town and doesn't come back for days?" she asked. "What would happen to you and me if Dad and Milo got lost in the storm, and they didn't get back for days and days? We would starve to death while we waited for them."

"Oh, Alice, we would not," I laughed. "We could have about eight bowls of oatmeal, and there's the apple cereal. And soup left over from last night. Anyway, this isn't like the blizzard Pa Ingalls got lost in. There's no snow, so you can see for miles. They'll find their way back."

"It howls just like a blizzard." Alice said, shivering beside me. Then she said, "I bet if we got very, very hungry, and we went down to Mr. de Hooch's house, he might feed us. Or he might call an orphanage to come get us." She shivered again and when I looked at her, I could see she didn't look altogether displeased with her latest idea. She likes to play orphanage.

"I wouldn't want Daddy to never come back," she said quickly. "But it might be kind of fun if we got to go to an orphanage just long enough to see what it looks like inside. And maybe see how they live. It would be interesting. Charlotte, I'm too hungry to wait for them any more. Do you mind if I put some of the cereal in a bowl? Without the milk, it looks like dog food. Since nobody else is here to care, I could put the bowl on the floor and pretend I'm a puppy. Just this once."

"Whatever," I said.

I wasn't worried about Dad and Milo, exactly, but I did feel a lot better when I saw them come back into view as they turned the corner from town. I noticed that the windmill blades weren't moving anymore, which should make their trip easier, but it still seemed to take a long time for them to get back to the house. When they finally

71

arrived, Dad flung open the door and thrust a net bag of groceries into my hand. "Here," he said, breathing hard. "Just put it down by the door and let us pass you the rest." He and Milo emptied both their saddlebags and then parked the bikes in the shed.

Alice and I had transferred most of the wet groceries from the hall into the kitchen by the time Dad and Milo came in the house. Their faces were red and they were soaked through.

"Stop," I commanded. "Shoes and socks and jackets off here." I almost regretted saying it, they looked so exhausted, but I hardened myself. I didn't want to have to wash mud off the floor later. I hung up their dripping jackets while they took off their shoes. Both of them were breathing too hard to talk and Milo was rubbing his ears.

"They're killing me now that I'm out of the wind," he said. "I hope I don't have to go out in anything like that again for a while."

"I'm beat," Dad admitted. "I think I could do with a cup of coffee, Charlotte. Could you start some? I'd like to have cereal too. Then I'm going back to bed. I want a nap."

"We thought you might be dead, or trapped in the storm, or something," Alice said.

"Well, our trip wasn't that dramatic, but it was no picnic for sure," Dad said, and Milo groaned in agreement, his hands still over his ears. "The ride to town wasn't enjoyable but it was all right until the rain hit. But coming back it was just crazy. We were riding against the wind and had to fight it every foot of the way. It probably would have been faster just to walk and push the bikes."

"But the windmill," I protested. "It isn't spinning anymore. I thought that meant that the wind wasn't blowing."

Dad snorted. "Haven't I taught you any better than

that? The wind is blowing so hard that they've locked the blades down to keep them from being blown straight into next week. Holland is famous for windmills because of the wind, but it's been so peaceful and quiet so far on this trip that you could almost forget about all that. Not today. Worse than Texas in a tornado." He disappeared into his room to change into dry clothes.

Milo lay down on the living room couch. "We got as much stuff as we could carry," he said, a little too loudly, because with his hands over his ears he couldn't tell how he sounded. "Doubles of some things like milk, so if the storm doesn't let up, we won't have to ride in tomorrow. Dad said we should start a pantry. We'll buy a little extra every time we go to the grocery store."

I put Alice to work wiping the rain off the groceries while I put them away. No wonder the food was wet. They'd probably stuffed the saddlebags so full they couldn't close them all the way. We now had bread, eggs, milk, frozen vegetables (which would make Mom happy when she heard about them), cheese, salami, hamburger, and about three jars each of jam and the magic sauce. Milk comes in boxes in the Netherlands, and there was an extra box of that as well. I put the extra groceries on a shelf in the laundry room.

Dad came out clean and dry. He poured himself a cup of coffee. Before he sat down to drink it, he used a few logs from the pile next to the fireplace to light a fire.

"The world's a cozy place even with weather like this as long as you've got plenty of groceries and a fire in the fireplace," Dad said. He got some cereal and sat down to enjoy his breakfast. We joined him.

"Now I want quiet," Dad said when we were finished. "I'm serious about the nap, and then I've got a lot of work to do. You kids need to keep yourselves occupied until lunch, and then for a while in the afternoon. I hope this rain stops soon."

But it didn't. It rained steadily for three days without a single break, although most of the wind had died down. We grew more irritable each day. Milo and I even started to fight over who got to go out for provisions with Dad. Braving the elements, no matter how wild, felt better than never leaving the house at all. Since Alice never got to go, she whined constantly for us to read to her and play games. Milo tried to get on the computer each time Dad stepped away from it. We had nothing to do but get on each other's nerves all day long. We became very good at it.

"It's my turn for the big chair!" Alice cried on the third day, when she went to the kitchen for a snack and found Milo sitting in the seat she'd vacated only a minute before. "You had it almost all day yesterday!"

"And I'm tired of watching the Tour de France," I complained. "Isn't there anything else on?"

"It's the perfect thing to watch here," Milo said. "You read the shirts and watch the flags on the screen and know exactly what's happening. I'm tired of the news, and I don't want to watch Russia's Toughest Prisons with Dutch subtitles running across it."

"Kids!" Dad said, looking up from the screen warningly.

"Milo, get out of my chair!" Though Alice had heard Dad, instead of finding something else to do, she went right on arguing, though she lowered her voice to a loud whisper. "I said, it's my turn to sit there!" She gave his shirt a yank.

"Forget it, squirt," Milo hissed, pushing back a little. "The chair's fair game whenever it's empty."

"Daddy!" Alice whined. "Make him give it to me. It's my turn!"

"That's it!" Dad wasn't yelling but he sounded like he

wanted to. "For three days I've tried to work and been interrupted by arguments every five minutes. I have got to get this report finished, and finished today. I've warned you, and I'm not going to do it again. Go outside. All of you. "

"In the rain?" Alice asked, shocked.

"Yes. In the rain. Put on your jackets and find some umbrellas." Dad combed his fingers through his hair in frustration. He crumpled up papers filled with diagrams and tossed them into the trash. "If you can't figure out a more productive way to use your time, stand under the thatch and argue there. But don't come back in this house for at least an hour."

We knew he meant it. Fortunately, it wasn't raining very hard. We put on our things and went outside.

The grass, always soft and springy, was so full of moisture that it tore apart when we stepped on it. Clearly, playing soccer was out. We put up the dartboard and played darts in the rain, chastened enough by Dad's irritation that we didn't argue as we did it. I overlooked the time Milo's dart wasn't quite a bull's eye when he claimed it was, and he generously counted the time my dart hit a high number but fell out immediately. We even came up with a scoring system for Alice, giving her points if she just managed to embed her dart in the tree bark.

We got so interested in the game, and we were already so wet that we didn't notice the weather at all until suddenly the sky cleared and the sun came out. At first, it didn't look like it would hold, but it got stronger and brighter by the minute. The birds began to chatter in the happy way they only do on a really glorious day.

Dad stepped outside, smiling. "Thanks, kids. I got the report done, and now I can take a break. Miss Alice, you're the only one who hasn't gotten away from here recently.

How about you and I have a date and go to the grocery store? Just the two of us?"

Alice beamed and ran to get a dry jacket, thrilled to be the one chosen to go with Dad. "Have fun, you two," Dad said to Milo and me. "Alice and I'll be back in an hour. What are you going to do while we're gone?"

"I'm going to try the canoe," Milo said. "Can you help me carry it down to the dock before you leave, Dad?"

That left the rowboat to me. Milo helped me wrestle the wet cover off. Maybe I could get out to the main canal by myself this time. Even though I hadn't rowed in a few days, the coordination I'd managed to achieve the other day came right back. The boat and I stayed smoothly in the middle of the canal, even when Milo darted past me in the canoe, which can go much faster than the rowboat. "Be careful," he called back to me a minute later. "There's a swan family up here hiding in the rushes. And the Mom is not happy to see me."

In a few minutes, I saw the swans myself. Actually, I heard them first. The swan mother was still honking angrily at Milo, but she made a sharp turn in the water when she realized how close I was. She hissed low in her throat, puffing out her wing feathers and jutting her long neck right toward my arm, and I was afraid for a minute she might attack me. I remembered I had oars if I needed them and yelled right back at her. She followed me down the canal, still scolding, and the babies scooted out of hiding.

As I approached Mr. de Hooch's house, I rowed as far as I could to the left side of the canal. Mr. de Hooch hadn't wasted any time getting outside in the sun either. And right next to him, in the other chair, sat the lady I'd seen the other day. Mr. de Hooch saw me and waved. His wife stood up immediately, and with only a quick glance at me, went down the path toward the house.

I couldn't understand what was so wrong about kids just rowing down a canal. She might have the biggest house in the neighborhood, but she didn't own the canal. Did she hate all Americans or something? Mr. de Hooch could have mentioned us to her and told her where we came from. Or was he really not as friendly as he had seemed last week? But no, he waved when he saw me.

"I see your rowing is improving, Charlotte," he said pleasantly.

"It's much better, thank you," I said. I couldn't help staring as his wife disappeared through the gate, and I blurted out, "Does your wife just not like kids near your house? We won't bother her, I promise."

"Mrs. de Hooch does not discriminate on the basis of age," he said, not smiling anymore.

That took me a minute to figure out. "Are you trying to say that she doesn't like anybody, even adults?"

He smiled again, but this time his eyes didn't match his mouth. "It just means she doesn't like being stared at, and that due to her own unfortunate life experience, she has learned not trust anyone who doesn't prove themselves first."

"But how do you prove yourself to her if she won't even stick around to look at you?" I asked.

"You have an excellent point, Charlotte," he said, "but I'm afraid that's the situation as it stands now."

"Well, goodbye," I said. I felt hurt, and my voice cracked and I probably sounded about as old as Alice. "You can tell her we'll really try not to bother her when we come past here. If we could go a different way in the boat, we would, but we can't, since it's a dead end on our side of the canal."

"I expect you children to use the boats and the canal in the ordinary way," Mr. de Hooch said. "In fact, I should be sorry not to see you out having fun from time to time. My wife would agree with me, even if she doesn't want to socialize." He waved, and I rowed away.

At first I just felt mad and humiliated that she would be so pointedly rude. I couldn't understand why it mattered what an elderly Dutch woman thought about me. But somehow it did, much more because she wouldn't give me the time of day than if she'd glared at me and looked back at her book. Why did I care whether she liked me?

It was because of that one moment when her eyes looked at mine. I hadn't expected what I saw there. I assumed she must be like some of the haughty, rich old ladies I see sometimes in Boston, walking their dogs at the park, but now I knew that couldn't be true. Her eyes were tired and sad, but not condescending or aloof. She looked like a kind person, a nice person, and her behavior didn't fit. I could tell it didn't annoy Mrs. de Hooch that we came by. It hurt her. I couldn't be angry anymore, and I couldn't forget about her either.

8

Time's a Wasting

Before my alarm had time to go off the next morning, I woke up to Dad hitting some pans together like a gong, and yelling all our names up the stairs.

"Milo! Charlotte! Alice! Rise and shine! The sun is out, and we're not going to waste this day sleeping!"

"Dad, it's barely seven-thirty," Milo called grumpily.

"Time's a wasting," Dad hollered. "Didn't you learn anything during the storm this past week? Make hay while the sun shines. The weather's supposed to be sunny today, and—can you believe it? Almost hot, all day long! No rain! No wind! No cold! We're going on an adventure! Who's in?"

"I am, Daddy!" Alice leaped out of bed like a natural early bird.

"I am, I guess," I said.

"I'm not," Milo said crossly. "Can we try again in about an hour?"

"No," Dad said, charging up the stairs to rouse Milo in person. "It was a purely rhetorical question. We're all in, and we're all in now. We've got exploring to do, and we aren't going to waste an hour of it." Milo groaned but the bed creaked and I heard water splashing in the sink in his room.

When we got downstairs after getting dressed, Dad was making sandwiches of rolls stuffed with a little bit of meat and a great deal of cheese. He put all of us to work finishing the lunch. Alice wrapped sandwiches in plastic, Milo filled water bottles, and I packed chocolate bars and the rest of the food in the saddlebags of the bikes outside.

"Aren't we even eating breakfast?" Alice asked hopefully. "We might faint while we ride or something, if we don't eat."

"I thought we could stop at the bakery in town for some pastries," Dad replied. "And we have another errand, too."

"What?" Alice asked.

"You'll see," Dad said. "It's something I know you're going to love." He wouldn't give another clue no matter how much she begged.

"Are we going to stop at the grocery store for more chocolate?" Alice asked.

"Nope. Better than that. You're going to love it."

Alice gasped. "I know what it is! We're going to go to a pet store and rent a dog for the rest of the summer!" Alice wants a dog more than just about anything else in the world. "Oh, please let that be it!"

Dad laughed. "Sorry, kiddo. Not that good. But better than chocolate."

Alice folded her arms. "The only thing better than chocolate would be a dog."

"Chip off the old block, on the chocolate, at least," Dad said. "You're my daughter for sure."

A few minutes later we were off. Not across the field this time, but toward the path beside a canal going to another village. This part of the bike path wove through a narrow ribbon of forest, with just enough room cut out for the cement path. Every now and then I caught a gleam of green water through the trees.

"Turn left up ahead," Dad called back to us. "We'll need to cross the bridge."

We emerged from the woods and turned, but before we could cross we heard a sound like a school bell. Slowly, the white bridge lifted up and collapsed in on itself neatly, like a folding chair, to let a sailboat through. We parked our bikes on the sidewalk and leaned over the railing in front of the bridge to watch while we waited.

"I'd love to see how these canals look from the water," Dad said as the boat came through. He whistled admiringly. "Gorgeous sailboat."

"That's just what I said the other day, Dad!" Milo said. "It's our neighbor's boat. They live a couple houses down. It's usually docked just around the bend in the canal."

Sure enough, it was the de Hooch's boat. Mr. de Hooch sat in the back, letting the sail out a little and then pulling it back in. He looked up, noticed us, and gave a friendly wave. All of us waved back. Mrs. de Hooch, busy at the wheel, glanced up and then straight back down again. I couldn't help enjoying the satisfaction of knowing that she couldn't get up and walk away from me.

"A dog! They have a sailor dog! Look at the darling thing," Alice cried, pointing to a small black dog that stood like a miniature wolf with his front legs on the railing, looking for all the world as if he owned the boat.

"I think he's smiling at me!" Alice said, skipping in place with excitement. "Oh, he's so adorable!"

As the boat passed, we could read the writing on the side and Alice tried to sound it out.

"The William? The Will Helmut? Who was Will Helmut?"

"It says *Wilhelmus*," Milo said. "It's a Dutch word, Alice."

"It's the Dutch national anthem," Dad said. "A good patriotic name for a Dutch boat." A red, white, and blue striped Dutch flag snapped crisply in the morning wind, and the de Hooch's and their boat disappeared down the canal.

"Have you seen them before?" Dad asked. "He seemed to recognize you all."

"He always says hello to me whenever I go past there," I said. "He's out on his dock a lot."

"He talks to me, too, about boats," Milo said. "I think he knows everything there is to know about boats and sailing."

"Well, be sure you don't bother the two of them," Dad said. "They're probably enjoying their retirement in peace and quiet."

Not both of them, I thought, but didn't say it out loud. The bridge folded back down and we pedaled across to the main street of the village. "Errand number one coming right up," Dad called.

"That's the bakery, right?" Milo said. "I'm starving!"

Dad shook his head. "We'll get to that next." He pulled to a stop in front of a bike shop, which was just opening for the day. "Miss Alice is getting her own wheels."

We parked the bikes, locked them, and went in to the shop. The elderly owner, dressed in a mechanic's coverall with his named stitched on it, greeted us pleasantly in Dutch.

"Do you speak English?" Dad asked.

We'd found that most people did, at least a little, but this man shook his head regretfully. "English bad. I call...*de vrouw*, my woman." He went to the phone, dialed, and spoke rapidly into the phone in Dutch. He gestured toward the rows of bikes. "Wait, look. She come."

"Me Tarzan, you Jane," mumbled Milo, too low for him to hear, and we giggled a little. In about five minutes, a businesslike woman came through the back door.

"What can we help you with?" she asked. "Do you want to buy or rent a bike?"

"We want to rent one until August, for this little girl here," Dad said, pointing to Alice. They talked about rental prices for a minute and Dad nodded, satisfied. "What do you have that would fit someone her size?"

"Hmmm, it is not much we have, for children," she said, frowning slightly as she led us to the smaller models. She gave Alice a long appraising glance. "There are two you may choose from. This one, and I think—this one."

One of the bicycles was pink, with a purple basket and sparkly things attached the wheels. Alice gasped out loud and ran to it. "This one," she cried. "Oh, I love this one."

Once she stood beside it, though, the lady shook her head regretfully. "No, too big, I am sorry. Too big for you. How about this one, instead?" Her hand rested on a bike the next size down. One look at it and Alice's chin began to tremble. This bike was much older than the pretty one and painted a strange orange color. It was clearly a boy's bike.

"No, not that one," she said. "I'm big enough for the other one. I know I am."

"Your legs, they are not quite long enough," the shop owner's wife said firmly. "It is not a good idea. I'm afraid you will smash into things since you are not big enough."

"Please, Dad," Alice begged. "Can't I just try it? It's so glittery. I would love to ride a bike like that."

"I think the lady may be right, Alice," Dad said. "You can't make your legs longer no matter how much you wish you could. The other one isn't good looking, but it will be safer for you."

"Just out here?" Alice pleaded. "Just to be sure?"

I felt sorry for her and knew she if she didn't see for herself that it wouldn't work, she'd be mourning the pink bicycle for the rest of our vacation. Every time she rode the orange bike, the pink would get better and better in her mind. Clearly Dad saw the same picture.

"Could we let her try it out in the driveway here?" he asked. I couldn't tell if the shop owner's wife was more worried about her bike getting ruined or Alice getting hurt because she hesitated before saying a reluctant yes. She wheeled the pink bike to the driveway and with difficulty, Alice climbed on.

"Maybe she can do it," I said to Dad, but Milo shook his head sadly. "She's gonna crash in about a minute," he said, sighing.

It was more like thirty seconds before Alice started to wobble and ran straight into the fence. Fortunately she wasn't badly hurt and neither was the bike. The shop owner's wife retrieved it and tactfully returned it to its place inside without saying a word. Dad bent down and picked up Alice.

"The other one isn't so bad, Alice," Milo lied. "It's a good, tough bike and it will be great on trails and through the mud. You wouldn't have wanted to get the other one dirty."

Even mentioning the pink bicycle was probably a bad idea. "I would have been really careful," Alice wept. "I would have cleaned it every night. The other one is so ugly. I hate it."

"You'll be safer on it and that's the most important thing," Dad said firmly. The shop owner's wife came through the door and Dad turned to her, still holding Alice. "We'll take the orange bike," he said.

They worked out the details. Dad pulled out his wallet, paid, and the shop owner's wife brought the bike outside. In the sun it looked, if anything, a little worse than it had in the shop. Alice's lip quivered as she got on. There was no doubt it fit her perfectly, and I think it made her a little mad to see how well she rode on it.

The bakery was just down the street. It was so tiny that only Dad and Alice went in to order while Milo and I stayed out with the bikes. In a few minutes, they reappeared with a white paper bag full of warm apple fritters. "Appelflappen," Dad told us. We didn't bother finding a spot to sit down and eat them, but devoured the whole bag standing right outside the bakery door.

"Man, those were great." Milo moaned, dusting off his hands. Alice didn't want to waste any of the candy sugar and licked it off her hands instead. She was going to be a sticky mess, but I didn't say anything because she looked extremely happy and seemed to have forgotten all about the orange bicycle leaning against the brick wall of the bakery.

Dad threw away the paper bag and got on his bike. We could feel another "Time's a wasting!" comment coming on, and mounted quickly before it came out of his mouth. "Where are we going?" I asked.

"According to the map in our kitchen, there are two polder mills a few miles west," Dad answered. "It's time to see a really truly Dutch windmill."

I thought the old windmills you see on the cover of books like Hans Brinker would be everywhere in the Netherlands, but so far we hadn't seen even one, although on the train from Amsterdam we passed several wind farms with row after row of modern white windmills. They were beautiful too, in a cool sort of way, but we've seen these plenty of times before because of Dad's work, and we all wanted to see the storybook ones.

Dad took off with Milo behind him and then Alice. I tried to stay behind Alice so I could be sure she was OK. It made me a little nervous to have her riding along the side of the road and not on a bike path, although there wasn't much traffic. It made me even more nervous that Dad didn't seem to worry about it. I knew it was probably a good thing Mom didn't know Alice was biking without a helmet. None of the rest of us have one either. I think maybe I've seen five helmets total since we got to the Netherlands. Nobody seems to care about that sort of thing over here.

In a few minutes, we left the town behind and now there were farms spread out on either side. It seemed like we could see for miles, and the sky went on forever. Boston is so crowded that it's the buildings you notice, not what's above them. But the Dutch sky is so blue it doesn't even look real, and there are no hills to spoil the view. It makes me homesick for Kansas City, although Kansas City isn't quite this lush green.

After about half an hour, we turned off the side road onto a much busier four-lane road. Dad turned around to check and make sure we were all still there. I was having a hard time pedaling slowly enough to keep going and stay behind Alice. Going fast is easy. Going slowly, all I could think about was how much sitting on the bike seat hurt after pedaling for an hour. But at least Alice had taken to the road like a champ. Every now and then I even heard some singing drifting back to me.

Dad stopped by the side of the road, and we caught up with him. "We're going to cross the highway up ahead," he told us, "then get on a bike path on the other side. Alice, how are you holding up?"

"Fine!" she said. "But I still wish I had the pink bike."

"Well, you're keeping up better than I thought you would," Dad said. "Give the bike a little credit too. He's doing his best for you."

"We'll call it the Great Pumpkin," Milo said. "It's sort of a Thanksgiving pumpkin pie orange. I've never seen that color on a bike before."

"And the Great Pumpkin it shall be," agreed Dad.

We did find our storybook windmill. It wasn't a working mill but seemed to be a family home. The windmill had no big picture window, obviously, but its little windows had scrubbed panes and window boxes with cheerful red geraniums underneath.

"I wish you could have rented this!" I told Dad. "We could write a book just about living in it!"

"They've got a swing set," Alice said. "I wish those kids would come out right now and ask me to play with them."

Milo was busy taking pictures of the windmill, so I'm glad no kids did come out. When he finished, we got back on the bikes, riding so far I was afraid I'd never be able to walk again once I got off. We stopped for our picnic lunch on a bench outside a stork sanctuary. Almost every tree up and down the road had an enormous messy nest up in the top of it, and above us a stork husband and wife had a noisy argument as we ate our sandwiches and chocolate. Our water bottles had turned warm and so had we.

"We've worked hard," Alice said. "I think we deserve ice cream."

She didn't have to beg for it because Dad was as hot as we were, and I think he probably wished we weren't so far from home. "Let's be on the lookout for a place to get some," he agreed.

It hurt like crazy to get back on the bike again. The one I'm using is a little too high for me and can't be adjusted down any more, and Milo's chain slips unpredictably. They aren't great bikes but they run, and since they came with our house, we didn't have to pay extra to rent them. Dad's bike is more comfortable than ours, but his brakes are tricky and he has to be careful not to stop too soon or too hard. Alice's bike, at least, only looks ugly.

Everything else on it works fine.

Spurred on by the thought of ice cream, we pedaled off with a will, out across more farmland and finally to a village. "There ought to be something here," Dad called. "A small café, at least."

We found a cafe, but it was closed. Milo got off his bike and tried the door to make sure it really was locked. It was.

"Who closes this early on a Saturday afternoon?" he asked crossly. "In the summer time? How far to the next village?"

Dad consulted the map. "Three miles," he said, and we all groaned. It turned out to be closer to four. The next village had a gas station, a fire station, a church, and an antique store, but no place to buy ice cream. We groaned again.

"I'm scared to ask," Milo said. "How long til the next one now?"

"Another three miles," Dad said reluctantly. We didn't bother taking time to whine because there was no point. We got back on silently and followed him out of the village on the bike path out of town. We'd gone a little more than two miles when we saw an old brick pub in the crossroads, with nothing else in sight. The wooden sign above the door said "Cafe de Vanhandel, Family Huizinga." It was worth a try. We parked our bikes outside.

"It looks a little creepy," I said apprehensively. "These windows are really dusty. That's not normal for Dutch people."

"How hard is it to dish out ice cream?" Milo pointed out. "I think we should see if they have any. It's not like they would make it here or anything. I'm about to die of exhaustion."

"Me too," Alice said, and Dad shrugged and went to

the green-painted front door. He tugged hard on it and then knocked but nothing happened.

"Maybe they don't use this one," Milo said. "I'll try the side door." He ran around to try it, but couldn't get it open either. "This place must be closed, too," he said. "Oh well. We're only, what, a mile from the next town?"

We bent over to unlock our bikes when the side door banged open and a sharp-looking woman stuck her head out the door, called out to us, and motioned for us to come in. She looked exactly like the kind of woman who would keep a dirty restaurant and every instinct in me said to pretend we didn't see her, get on our bikes fast, and get out of there. As much as Milo wanted ice cream, even he hesitated, but she called to us again, more impatiently this time.

"Someone knocked and pulled on the front door, but didn't come inside. Why would they do that?" She peered down her long nose at us and shook her head like it was the dumbest thing she'd ever heard of anyone doing. I'm not sure why any of us followed her into the building. Alice clung to my hand and tried to pull me back through the still open door.

"Do we just scream American?" Milo said into my ear. "How did she know to speak English to us before we said anything? Something's off about this place." He made a slicing motion under his throat and Dad frowned hard at him.

"You can come in here," the woman said ungraciously, pointing to the back room. "Sit down. Make yourselves comfortable." The last part sure didn't sound sincere. She turned on her heel and left us there to find our own seats.

"Quick, let's get out of here, Daddy," Alice begged. "I don't like that lady. I don't like this place." Milo was closest to the door, and tried to open it. "Dad, I think she locked us in," he hissed in a panic. "I can't get it open. What do we do?"

Before Dad could answer, the woman reappeared in the doorway. "I said, you can sit down," she said, severely. "I thought you were hungry. I thought you wanted something to eat."

Come on, Dad, I thought. *This is where you tell her that we were lost and we just needed directions to the next town. And then we leave, right now.*

But Dad is much too honest to lie like that. We all sat down. "We just want some ice cream," he told her. "How much for a small cone?"

The price she quoted was double the cost of ice cream anywhere else, but it was as though she'd cast an evil spell on Dad. He looked unhappy but ordered four cones.

"Why did we stay?" I asked him in amazement. The red checked oilcloth on the table had cracks in it, and the condiments looked as though they hadn't been used or changed in twenty years. The few grains of rice in the saltshaker were yellow with age and when I turned the pepper shaker over, nothing moved inside. "Gross!" I said, putting it back down on the table next to a dead fly.

"What are those things all over the walls?" Alice asked suspiciously. "Are they to hit people with?"

Ranged around every available area of the wall in the room was a collection of what appeared to be antique soup ladles. Alice's lips moved quietly. She was counting them. "Ten, eleven, twelve, thirteen..."

"We're all set if we want to be a family band," Milo said, pointing to a folding table on which rested a half dozen accordions in various sizes.

"And we're all set if we need clothes," I responded, pointing to the boxes underneath the table, which spilled over with a collection of raggedy items which had either just come from a thrift store or would soon be on its way to one. Clearly this room didn't usually serve as a restaurant dining room. "Why did she put us in here all alone, Dad?" I asked.

Milo didn't answer but made the slicing motion under his throat again. "Does anybody have anything we can use as a weapon if we need it?" he asked. "I can swing my camera on its strap and clock her with it if I have to, but that's a last resort. I don't want to break it on someone like her."

"We are just fine," Dad said. "She's a little eccentric, and this place will give us some authentic local color, that's all. I'm sure we don't need to worry about defending ourselves."

"But if we don't worry about it, who else will?" Milo asked reasonably. "Nobody in the world knows we're even in this town. Even Mom doesn't know where we are exactly today. That woman could poison us and dispose of our bodies in the basement and nobody would ever trace us here. It's the perfect crime."

Just as he finished saying it, the woman walked through the door carrying two ice cream cones, which she shoved toward Dad and Alice. She curled her lip and frowned at Milo. Who knew how much of his little speech she'd heard. She turned without a word and went back to the kitchen.

Alice stared at the cone in her hand. The ice cream looked thick and velvety. "Is it safe to eat, do you think?" she whispered to Dad, who stared down at his cone momentarily before taking a bite. He rolled his eyes and swallowed in exaggerated appreciation. Then his eyes bulged and he grabbed his throat with one hand, his tongue lolling out. Alice squealed in fear and Milo jumped.

"Got you," Dad said, grinning at Milo. "It's great ice cream, just great. Creamy. Delicious. Go ahead and enjoy it, Alice." She sighed in relief and started licking the drips on the side of her cone.

The woman came into the room and handed a cone to me. She averted her eyes before handing Milo his, and then slapped the bill next to Dad's place and left without saying a word.

"I think she hates me," Milo said, looking nervously at the cone. "I'm not sure I should eat this. Even if yours aren't poisoned, mine might be."

"I'll take that chance if you don't want it," Dad said reaching for the cone, but at this Milo cautiously took a bite.

"It tastes all right," he conceded. "But I'm not sure that means anything. You don't always taste poison." But I could tell he was weakening as he watched the rest of us enjoying ours. The ice cream tasted like rich custard, and I almost forgot where I was until I heard Alice softly counting again.

"Forty-four, forty-five, forty-six..."

"Why would any sane person have forty-six ladles?" Milo asked. "I'm telling you, Mom and Grandma Sybil are going to wonder whatever happened to us, but someday they'll be watching a crime show about a crazy Dutch lady and the restaurant she used to lure traveler after traveler to an untimely death. And then, they'll know."

We burst into giggles at this, but mine ended abruptly when I remembered the locked door. "How are we going to get out of here, Dad?" I asked uncertainly.

"We'll walk out to the front," Dad said. "I've got to pay the bill anyway. Come on, let's go."

"I've got to go to the bathroom," Alice said, as we stood up.

"Alice, can't it wait?" I asked.

"We'll wait right outside the door," Dad assured me more than Alice. "Go in with her, Charlotte," he said when we reached the bathroom door.

We went inside the dark ladies' room and I groped around on the wall for a light. "Check the other side," I hissed to Alice, and she slid her hand obediently across the wall.

"I don't think there's a light switch over here," she said. "Maybe I can't reach high enough."

"Wait, I think I found it," I said, and flipped the switch. It came on with only about the intensity of a nightlight, but that was enough light for us to realize that we weren't in any ordinary bathroom. Not that I was expecting one.

"Why is there a bicycle for two people in here?" Alice whispered to me. "I've never seen one of those in a bathroom before, have you?"

"I've never seen a toilet like that before," I whispered back. It was elevated like a throne. I moved back toward the door and bumped into the sink, knocking one of about fifteen bottles of hairspray and a few curlers onto the floor.

"I think the lady lives in this building, and this is her bathroom," I told Alice. The light flickered weirdly and went out for a few seconds. Alice grabbed my hand and didn't let go even after it turned back on. When it did I noticed a penciled sign attached to the wall, with a basket underneath. I could read just enough Dutch to know that it said something like, "Fifty cents, please."

"How bad do you have to use the bathroom," I asked, pointing to the sign. "It costs fifty cents."

"They should pay people who are brave enough to use this bathroom!" Alice said indignantly. "I would use the bushes first." She stomped to the door and I turned off the light.

"There's a bike in there?" Milo asked, interested.

"You could hear us whispering?" I asked, shocked.

"The acoustics must be awesome," Dad said, grinning.

"Or it's not acoustics," Milo said. "The room is bugged and they play it from a speaker right outside. Can we go now, Dad?"

We almost stampeded to the front room and stopped short.

Was it a movie set or a time machine? The main eating area of the pub looked as though it hadn't been redecorated since World War II. Smoke-stained brown wallpaper clung in patches to the wall. The enormous built in sideboard was crammed full of old pewter and dishes. Even on this warm June day, all the windows and shades were closed, and a fire burned in a fireplace that stretched across part of one wall. But what really got our attention was the pine table in the middle of the room, where about a dozen men, who looked as though they might have been in their prime at the same time the restaurant was last made over, sat smoking and playing cards. They froze when they heard us come in, and turned as one to stare at us malevolently.

That did it. I bolted for the door, but it didn't open. I gave it a second mighty and frantic tug, and when it flew open I ran outside, not caring what anyone thought. Milo and Alice were right behind me. With a hard bang, Milo pulled the door shut behind us and we rushed to our bikes and jumped on, waiting for Dad to finish paying the bill. A minute later he sprinted out, jumped on his own bike, and led us to the road. Nobody said a word for about five minutes. We just pedaled hard to put as much space as we could between us and the restaurant.

Up ahead, Dad began to laugh. Then we were all laughing, and we laughed so hard we cried and had to pull the bikes over.

"You know what?" Dad gasped. "They were as scared of us as we were of them. That's what's so funny. They're gambling in there—that's betting, Alice. Probably illegally. That's why she locked us in, and that's why she put us in the back room."

"Let's stop at a police station and turn them in," Milo said. "I think gambling is just the tip of the iceberg. She could be the granddaughter of an axe murderer or something."

"She sells good ice cream, though," Alice said. "Can we go back tomorrow?"

"No, Alice," Dad said, still laughing. "I think one ice cream cone at that restaurant is enough for one summer."

9

Jaap

During the next few weeks, the weather dried up like it had forgotten how to rain. We took more bike trips when Dad wasn't working, and he helped us string up a hammock next to the canal. Alice and I took turns with it. Now that Milo's hand had healed up, we hardly ever saw him. He spent every spare minute out on the canal in the canoe. When Mom heard on Skype how far he could go, she insisted he wear a life jacket.

"Nobody around here does," he mumbled. "Just like nobody around here wears helmets. And we don't hear about any accidents."

"You don't hear about any accidents because you can't read the newspaper and you can't understand the TV news," Mom snapped. "It's hard enough for me to have you children a continent away without knowing my only son might drown in a Dutch canal. You can do at least this for me, Milo. Wear a life jacket."

I could tell Dad sympathized with Milo. "Meg," he soothed, "these canals aren't really all that deep, and certainly not wide. Nobody's going to drown. Milo's a good swimmer, and he'd easily be able to get to the side."

"Is it really too much to ask," Mom asked, "for something that would give me some peace of mind when I can't be with my children?" There was an uncomfortable silence all around.

"It's not going so well there, is it?" Dad asked

sympathetically. "Come on, Meg, it's not like you to be this irritable."

Mom sighed. "It's pretty rough. Medically, Mama's doing all right. The doctor says her numbers are right where they should be in this phase of her treatment. It's just hard. She handled the first round like a champ—insisting we go out to eat afterward or for a walk. She walked so fast she almost left me in the dust."

"That sure sounds like Grandma Sybil," Alice said, and we all agreed.

"Well, it didn't last," Mom said. "Every day she got a little slower, and now she's coming straight home to bed. She turns off the lights and sleeps the rest of the day, and then I hear her roaming around half the night, so I can't sleep, either. She insists she feels fine but she has circles like bruises under her eyes, and every tiny thing sets her off. She especially hates having me cook in her kitchen."

"She probably hates that you use good stuff like butter and red meat," I said, but Mom shook her head.

"I'm making everything the way she wants it, but she's just mad she can't be doing it herself. Honestly, so am I. I'm working my fingers to the bone to try to please her, but nobody can right now. She is the best mother in the world, when she's feeling well and in control. When she's not, well..."

"Heaven help anyone around her," Dad supplied. "I get the picture. You're a saint, Meg. You know we're praying, but we'll pray even harder."

"I miss you all so much, and I want to be there with you," Mom said, tearing up. "That doesn't help. But let's not talk about that anymore. Tell me what you've been doing. Cheer me up."

"We've got the perfect story for you," Dad said, grinning. "Tell her about the ice cream adventure, kids."

Soon we were all laughing, even Mom, and she was still smiling when we said goodbye.

Telling Mom about the restaurant reminded me that I hadn't written about it in Annabeth's journal yet. I went out to the hammock to write and draw. I thought Alice was already in the back yard, and half expected to have to fight her for the hammock, but she wasn't there. I settled into the cushions and had just begun to draw when I heard a dog barking. I looked over the canal to the bike path, but I didn't see anyone out walking a dog.

We know most of the dog owners around here by sight now. Every night a lady jogs past with a Labrador retriever. Early in the morning, while I'm making breakfast, I usually see a man walking two King Charles spaniels. They're both eager and sort of naughty dogs, and they get tangled up a lot, and he has to straighten them out. Sometimes there's a little friendly yelling. And then there's the tall elderly lady who sort of floats along with her big poodle. It's hard not to laugh when I watch the two of them because their hair matches perfectly.

But none of the regulars were on the bike path in either direction. I settled back down to finish my picture and was just putting the final touches on Mrs. Huizenga's amazing ladle collection when I heard more barking around the side of the house, followed by shushing and thumping noises. I closed my journal and slid out of the hammock to investigate.

Alice must have heard me coming because one of the patio chairs scraped across the tiles, and I found her sitting at the table, whistling so innocently that I knew she was up to something.

"Come on, Alice, spill. Where's the dog I just heard barking, and where did you get it?"

"I don't see any dog," Alice said, eyes wide.

"I don't see one either," I said, "but we both know it was there. Where did you put it?"

"I just want to play with him for a little bit longer," Alice begged. "Can't you pretend you didn't hear him and let us finish our circus? Then I'll take him home."

"Wait. You know this dog?" I asked.

"I think so," Alice said. "He looks like the same little dog we saw on Mr. de Hooch's boat yesterday. He's black with a fancy little feathery tail. He was sitting on the patio when I came outside. I think he was bored and wanted to play. He's very good at tricks. He jumped over that big bucket, and I only had to show him one time how to do it. He already knows how to beg on his hind legs, and he walks right next to me. I just love him."

I had to ask the obvious question. "Where did you put him, Alice?"

She sighed. "OK, I will show you, but I thought you might have figured that out by now because that big bucket over there keeps walking to different places in the yard."

Sure enough, the next moment an upside-down green bucket moved slightly to the left. Alice ran over and lifted it up to reveal the dog, and when she put it down next to him, he backed up a little and leaped lightly over it. His bright black eyes looked up at Alice with obvious pleasure, and he panted, quivering with excitement as he waited for her next command.

"The only trouble," Alice explained to me, "is that he's used to being told what to do in Dutch, and he isn't always sure what I want in English. So the language thing is kind of a problem for us, but it seems like he can almost guess what I want, he's so smart. He always does something when I tell him to, even if it's not the right thing."

I knelt down on the grass and patted the little dog, and he licked my hand. His fur had the soft, clean sheen that only a really well-cared for dog's coat does. "Come on, Alice," I said, "we need to take him back. You can see they love him a lot, and maybe they know he's missing now. They might be worried."

"You're right," Alice agreed reluctantly. "Come on, Snap. I'm calling him that because he does things when I snap my fingers." She snapped them now and the dog immediately followed us through the yard to the road out front.

"I wish we could keep him," Alice said. "He's just the kind of dog I've always wanted. I keep asking and asking, but Mom and Dad keep saying no. Do you think once we move to Oregon, they might say yes about getting a dog?"

I shook my head. "I don't think so, Alice. We always rent because we move so much. And most rental places don't want to take pets. In Boston, we haven't even had a yard. If you don't have a yard, it's much harder to have a dog, even if there's a dog park nearby. Dogs need space to run and play every day."

"Just like kids do," Alice said, and she slowed down until she was practically walking backwards so she could keep the dog a little longer. "Charlotte, do you ever wish we lived in one house, our own house, so we could have our own yard and our own dog? I sure do."

"All the time," I said. "Our own house, with a bedroom I could paint any color I wanted. I want to live there long enough that there's junk in the closet and boxes of old stuff in the attic. And a dog would be really great too." I reached out and took Alice's hand. "But that's not now and he's not ours."

We got to the end of the road to what I assumed must be the de Hooch's driveway because it was the last one. It curved sharply to the right. Birch trees grew thickly on either side of the drive, and we couldn't see either the road behind us or a house ahead. A car came toward us and we jumped back into the trees. It was a long black limousine and it looked important.

"Maybe Mr. and Mrs. de Hooch are in there," Alice said hopefully. "And we can keep Snap a little longer."

"No, I don't think so," I said. "I couldn't see inside too well, since the windows were dark, but the shapes of the people were wrong to be them. Sorry, Alice."

The longer we walked down the driveway without seeing a house, the less comfortable I felt being there, but after a few minutes we came to the same kind of brick and iron fence that stood in the back yard. A green painted gate blocked the rest of the driveway.

"Well, fella, how are we going to get you back?" I asked the dog, and he panted and smiled up at me, content to let me figure it out.

"We could walk all the way around," Alice said. "I bet Mr. de Hooch is sitting in the back. Come on, Snap," she said, and followed the fence toward the back. After a minute she stopped, grabbed the railing, and yelled through the fence. "Hey, Mrs. Lady, I have your dog. He came to visit me, but we brought him back."

Of course, Mrs. de Hooch would be the one outside, I groaned to myself. *And Alice has no idea how to be tactful.*

As I got closer, I could see Mrs. de Hooch hesitate, torn between wanting her dog back and not wanting to talk to us. The dog won out, and she came over to where Alice stood.

"He's so cute," Alice said, giving her a big smile and not seeming to care that she didn't get one in return. "And so smart too. He makes a good circus dog. What kind is he? And what is his name?"

I was glad I'd taken time to braid Alice's hair this morning, because with her pigtails and twirly pink skirt she looked irresistibly cute. Even Mrs. de Hooch seemed to soften a tiny bit because she looked right at Alice when she answered her.

"He is a Schipperke," she said, and I noticed her English had a lot more of a Dutch accent than her husband's did. "And his name is Jaap."

"Snap?" Alice cried. "That's what I called him."

"No, it is a Dutch name," Mrs. de Hooch corrected. "Jaap. The beginning sound is like your 'y' and is more like 'mop' than 'snap.' He will come around the fence when I call. We had just realized he was gone. Thank you for bringing him back."

And you can both go home now, I think she might have wanted to add, but she was too polite to do so. Alice leaned down and gave the dog a hug. "Goodbye, Snap-Jaap. You can come visit me anytime." She stood up again and asked, confidingly, "Don't you just have fun with him every single minute? I would, if I had a dog like him. He's perfect."

This time Mrs. de Hooch did smile a little and it looked real. "Yes," she said. "He is a wonderful little friend, and we're very lucky to have him." She said something to the dog in Dutch and Jaap took off along the fence to the gate.

"Goodbye," Alice called, and we started back down the tree-lined driveway.

"I think we are making some progress with that woman," Alice said, satisfied.

I laughed. "Well, we know what she'll talk about, anyway. Her dog."

At supper that night, Dad rapped on the table. "Let this meeting come to order," he said. "In other words, this is an official discussion, and I need for you to be quiet and pay attention."

Milo made a goofy salute and Alice said, "Aye, aye, Captain!" We're used to Dad's meetings.

"Thank you," Dad said, bowing in his chair. "All right. I've got to go to Amsterdam tomorrow. It's a lunch meeting and it shouldn't last long, so I can take the train down there and be back before dinner. Since the restaurant is on the other side of town from the office building, there's not really a place for you three to be while we're talking. I think you can stay here by yourselves for that long, but we need to have a few rules."

"We have plenty of rules already," Milo protested. "Dad, we'll behave ourselves. You don't have to make up a bunch of rules for tomorrow."

"Your first day alone here did not inspire me with confidence," Dad said. "If that cut on your hand had been just a little deeper, Milo, you would have needed stitches. Thank goodness your Mom never found out about it. And I don't think she'd be too thrilled that I'm leaving you alone tomorrow, either. So here is Rule Number One. Don't tell her."

"You want us to lie to Mommy?" Alice looked horrified, and Dad backtracked hastily.

"Of course I don't want you to lie to her. If she happens to ask you directly, tell her. But let's not give her something to worry about until it's safely over. All right, Rule Number Two. Call me if you have an emergency."

"How will we do that?" Milo asked. "We haven't got a phone."

Dad tossed a new cell phone across the table to Milo, whose eyes lit up. Milo has wanted a phone forever. "You've got one now," Dad said. "It's a prepaid phone with an hour's worth of minutes on it. I bought it in town this afternoon and programmed my number in. You can call me any time you need to. I also looked up the number for the local ambulance service and programmed that in as well."

He showed us how the phone worked. "Milo, you're in charge of this. It needs to be on you if you leave the house. But I'd really rather you three don't leave the yard tomorrow unless you absolutely have to. That's Rule Number Three."

"But if we don't leave the yard," I said, "we'll be bored. And when we're bored, we fight."

"And when we fight, we get hurt," Alice finished.

"So you see, it's just as dangerous to keep us here as to let us roam," Milo agreed.

"Oh, but you're not going to fight," Dad said calmly. "Because that's Rule Number Four. Absolutely no fighting at all, for any reason. You will be kind and considerate to each other all day long. Period. The End."

"I don't think we can do that," Alice said, worried. "A whole day? How?"

"You just will, or else," Dad said. "If I come home and find you maimed or wounded due to fighting, you don't even want to know what's going to happen. OK, then. Moving right along. To keep you from having to leave the house for groceries, we will all go to the store together first thing tomorrow morning. Smit's opens at eight, and we will be at the grocery store, parking our bicycles, at precisely eight o'clock."

We all groaned, and Dad grinned. "To make up for the fact that you poor, put-upon children must be up and out so early, we will pick up some pastries at the bakery afterwards. I understand there is also a cherry version of the delightful appelflappen we had the other day." We cheered at this news.

"All right. One more rule. Milo is in charge. You do what he says, and I'm going to call him twice during the day to make sure you do. And Milo, don't let it go to your head. When I get home, I'm going to ask your sisters how you treated them, and I don't want to find out that you were bossing them around any more than is truly necessary. Got it?"

"Yes, sir," Milo said, and Dad looked meaningfully at Alice and me. "Don't you hassle your brother, either. Got that?" We did.

"I wish we could go back to Amsterdam with you, Daddy," Alice said. "I want to visit my friends, those lizards. They've probably forgotten their names by now."

"I know," Dad said. "But you'll have to remind them another time."

Everything worked like clockwork the next morning. We got our groceries, and our pastries (the cherry wasn't as good as apple, we decided), and Dad got us safely settled in at home before he left for the bus stop. He gave each of us a hug goodbye, even Milo.

"This seems kind of formal for a couple of hours, Dad," Milo said, embarrassed. "I promise everything will be OK. Have a good meeting."

"You're sure you know how to use the phone?" Dad asked.

"Dad, we all know how to use the phone," I said. "You're beginning to sound like Mom."

"You're right," Dad laughed. "It's time for me to go. See you at dinner time, kids." He waved goodbye and rode out of the yard on his bike.

"Stuck here all day and it's not even raining," Milo said sadly once Dad was out of sight.

"I know," I said. "Let's make a list of all the things that we want to do during the rest of the summer, and see if there are any we can do today."

"Anything I really want to do is away from here," Milo said. "I want to ride to every village within a ten mile radius. I want to canoe down every canal within a ten mile radius. That's pretty much it."

"I want to sleep in the rowboat," Alice said, unexpectedly. "I would put the hammock cushions in the boat and take my pillow out there. And put the cover on, in case it rains, but maybe roll it down a little for air."

I was impressed at how she'd figured it all out. "I bet that would be a fun way to spend the night," I said.

"Then you can be the one to be out there with me," Alice said, and bowed as if she were bestowing a gift.

"That's another thing we can't do during the day today," I said. "But we should ask Dad about it when he comes home. I'm sure he'd let us."

"This conversation is a waste of time as far as finding something to do," Milo said. "Let's go play soccer. We can do that in the yard, and the ground is finally dry enough that we won't tear up the grass."

"And after that, we can play darts," Alice agreed. "We could just play different games all day long."

"And keep a running score for points from game to game," I said. "The losers can both chip in to buy the winner a chocolate bar when we go to the store the next time."

This idea even pleased Milo. "I think we should fix the points somehow so that Alice gets more than we both do," he said magnanimously. "That will give her a level playing field. It's more fun if everybody has a chance."

This was so unlike Milo that I wondered if power had gone to his head, only in a good way. Maybe we really could get through this day without fighting. "I think we should have points for winning and also for good behavior," I said.

"That will make us want to be nice, which would keep us from being mad at each other."

"Which would keep Dad from being mad at us!" Alice exclaimed. "Great idea, Charlotte."

We made a point sheet and I even decorated it with little doodles around the edges, and we stood around for a minute admiring it and feeling good about ourselves, and about how well the day was going to go.

10

Camping

Our soccer game was intense. Alice and I played against Milo. "Too bad Jaap didn't come down today," Alice said. "He and I could be a team. He'd be really good at soccer, I think."

"He'd be really good at getting the ball out of the canal too," I said. "Better than we are." We'd had to call four time-outs to fish the ball out with one of the canoe paddles. Alice insisted on trying to retrieve it the third time we accidentally kicked it in, and she leaned out too far.

"Alice, get back," Milo yelled. He almost caught her shirt before she fell in but didn't quite get to her in time.

Alice made a squealing sound when she hit the water, but surfaced with a fist pump. She spit out water. "Finally!" she gasped. "Finally, I fell into the canal! I've been wanting to do that since we got here!"

Milo rolled his eyes at me, and we hauled Alice out of the water and wrung as much of it out of her clothes as we could before marching her in the house to get a shower and change. That was the end of the soccer game.

"We definitely won," Alice shouted through the bathroom door to Milo. "We had four goals and you only had two."

"That one where it went over the woodpile and through the woods didn't count," Milo hollered back. "It was a foul."

"We still had more points," I said. "Even if you take

that one out. So that's one point each for Alice and me."

I had to help Alice wash her hair. Alice's hair is high-maintenance, long and curly, and it snarls terribly when it's wet. "Ow, you're killing me," she wailed about seventeen times in five minutes.

"Well, it's your own fault," I said. "You know and I know that you were sort of hoping you'd fall in the canal. You leaned out a lot farther than you had to in order to get that ball."

Alice giggled. "I thought Daddy might be a little mad if he had to stop working to clean me up, and suddenly I remembered he wasn't here, so it might be a good day to do it when it wouldn't bother him at all."

I gave her a little spank. "Well, now you've done it and know what it feels like, so don't do it again. Dad made us promise we wouldn't get hurt while he was gone, remember?"

"Oh, I won't do it again ever," Alice said positively. "It's kind of gross down there, actually. It's all muddy and squooshy at the bottom, with lots of roots and things all the way through the water. And it's cold!"

"Aren't you two ever going to be through prettying Alice up?" Milo called. "I thought we were going to play darts next. I've been waiting for half an hour!"

We hurried up and went outside. Milo is very good at darts, and after losing the soccer game, he was determined to win this. I think he'd been practicing the entire time I was working on Alice's hair. His arm slammed back and forth in one fluid movement with unerring accuracy, and he kept nailing darts right into the first ring. In fact, the only throw he missed was when the phone rang from inside his pocket. He dropped his dart on the ground to pull it out.

"Oh, hi, Dad," he said. "You made it in? Great. We're out in the yard playing darts. Yes, of course we're all still alive! We have all our eyes, and nobody's even wet." He mouthed the word "anymore" and Alice and I giggled nearly loud enough for Dad to hear. "We played soccer a little while ago. Alice and Charlotte beat me, but that was two against one. I'm killing them in darts."

Dad talked to each of us for a few seconds, mostly to confirm we were alive. When he was satisfied on that point, he said goodbye and we went back to our game. But it didn't go so well for Alice, who kept missing the target, and even the tree. She pouted that the game wasn't fair and stomped into the house. We docked a point for bad behavior, which made her madder, and she kicked the brick wall and hurt her foot. Milo made her sit in a chair until lunch and told her she'd need to rest after lunch because she was being a bad sport.

"This could be a long day," Milo said to me as we started assembling bread and cheese sandwiches.

"We were doing so well all morning," I said. "What happened?"

"Listen up over there, squirt," Milo called to Alice. "We're going to pretend that didn't happen. You have another chance to straighten up, and if you do I won't mention it to Dad. Keep sulking, though, and it will be the main topic of our next phone conversation. Understand?"

"Maybe," Alice said. Her arms were firmly crossed over her chest and her attitude obviously hadn't changed at all.

"No, you don't understand," I said. "When Dad calls, I'm going to tell him Milo is right and you're being bratty. I'm pretty sure you don't want me to have to tell him that."

Alice immediately uncrossed her arms and gave us both a fake but brilliant smile. "I'm happy now," she assured us through lips tight from smiling.

Milo decided not to push it. "All right," he said.

"Keep it that way. Get up and come over here for lunch."

"What are we doing after lunch?" Alice asked, getting up.

"Something quieter than darts or soccer," Milo replied. "Let's have a Monopoly championship." We ate lunch and then began to play. About an hour into our game the phone rang again.

"Yes, Dad, everything's fine here," Milo said. "Boringly fine, actually. We're playing Monopoly. Alice is winning. She has all the green properties, and all the red and orange ones, and the railroads. With hotels. Charlotte is out and I probably will be too on the next turn. Sure, I'll put it on speaker." Milo punched the button.

"Hi Alice, Charlotte," we heard Dad say. "I'm so proud of you guys. Thanks for behaving for Milo. Listen, I've got a little bit of an emergency here. The CEO got a call from a bigger company in California that wants to buy part of the research I've been doing during the last few weeks. It means a bonus for me and one for the company, too."

"That's great, Dad!" I said. He'd been worried about whether the Dutch company would like his work.

"Thanks," Dad said. That's the good news, but they're putting a rush on it and the CEO wants to have another meeting first thing in the morning. I should have brought you three in with me today. I was going to tell him I wouldn't be able to meet until later in the afternoon tomorrow, so I could get home to bring you guys back in with me, but if things are going that well, do you think you'd be OK alone overnight? It's not something we'd ever do in Boston, but it's probably safe enough out there in the country. What do you say?"

On one hand it sounded like the most exciting thing ever to stay alone but scary, too, and I was about to say I'd rather not when Milo said firmly, "Sure, Dad. We can totally handle it. Stay there and we'll see you tomorrow."

"Thanks," Dad said gratefully. "I'll be done by ten and home just after lunch. I've got another meeting in a couple days, but I've learned my lesson. If I go to Amsterdam, you go to Amsterdam. I hope Mom doesn't kill me when she finds out about this, but I'm sure you'll be fine. Do we need to run through Rules One through Five again?"

"No, Dad," we chorused.

"Good. I didn't think so. I'll make it up to you when I get home, I promise. I've got a great bike trip planned. And since you're helping me earn this bonus, I'm going to pass a little of it on to you in souvenir money. I know Alice has been dying for wooden shoes. You can each get a pair, or have the same amount of money to buy something else you might want."

"Daddy, thanks!" Alice cried. She's stopped at every souvenir place we've been to so far, trying out wooden shoes. She's figured out her Dutch shoe size and everything, but didn't have enough euros to buy them.

"You should be fine for groceries," Dad continued. "I'd still like you to stay on the property. Be safe. Bye, kids." He hung up. We just sat there, not saying anything.

"I really wish Daddy would come home tonight," Alice finally said. Her lip trembled a little bit.

"Me too," I confessed.

"That's three of us," Milo said. "But come on, let's make the most of it. Alice, you get a point for winning Monopoly." He went to the list and added it. "We now have a three way tie. No more games for now, though. I just had a fabulously brilliant idea."

"What?" I asked, suspicious that his idea might include us cleaning his room or becoming his slaves until

Dad got home.

"Let's camp out tonight. Like Dad says, it's perfectly safe here. Nobody's even staying in the house next door this week, so we wouldn't bother anyone. Alice wants to sleep in the rowboat, and you can sleep in there with her. I'll get out that old tent from the storage room and sleep in that."

"I'm not sure Dad would approve of this," I said.

"Dad only said not to go out of the yard," Milo said. "And we won't. It's perfectly safe. The rowboat is built like a tank, so it's not going to sink or anything, and it's been so dry lately there's not a speck of water in it. There's a storm coming tomorrow afternoon and it's supposed to rain most of next week, so if we don't camp out tonight, we won't be able to do it for a long time. I'm sure Dad would want us to make hay while the sun shines. That's what he's always telling us."

"We could call and ask him," I said, giggling, because somehow I knew Dad would not apply his favorite saying to this particular situation. Alice looked thrilled and excited, and scurried straight to the storage room to get out the hammock cushions and try them out in the rowboat.

I helped Milo pull the tent down from the rafters, and we shook it hard to get the dust off and then set it up to air out. The tent hadn't been used in years, and I wrinkled my nose at the musty smell.

By suppertime the smell was bearable, and Milo moved in. He took some lounge cushions to make a ground pad, and brought the eiderdown from his bed to use as a sleeping bag.

"We can't light a campfire," Milo said. "But once we've cooked dinner, let's eat it outside, to make it more like camping."

Because of the risk of fire to the thatched roof, Dad

and Mom had signed an agreement not to light any matches outside. So we fried sausages on the stovetop inside, and warmed up some mashed potatoes. We added apples to our plates so we could reassure Dad that we'd eaten a balanced meal, and then took our dinner outside to a blanket spread on the ground next to Milo's tent.

For a while we didn't say anything, just ate quietly. We watched the rowboat bob up and down on the canal and waved to a group of bikers who rode past on the path beyond it. Milo put his plate down and then lay back on the blanket. "This is the life," he said, very contentedly for Milo. "I wish Dad could work here for longer than just this summer. I'm not in any hurry to go home."

"Wherever that is anymore," I said. "Have we got one?"

"Home is where the heart is," Milo said, sort of laughing while he quoted Mom's favorite saying.

"Bloom where you're planted, and all that," I said. "That's easy for Dad to say, but I'd love to stay planted somewhere like this."

"Somewhere we could have a yard, for a dog exactly like Jaap," Alice said.

"I wonder what Oregon will be like," I said.

"Gloomy," Milo answered. "According to Wikipedia, it's cloudy two hundred and one days a year."

"It's supposed to be beautiful, though," I said. "You can take lots of pictures there. And it should be a good place for boating too." Milo just grunted.

It takes a long time for it to get dark in the Netherlands in the summer since it's so far north. The light doesn't completely disappear until way past Alice's bedtime. We went back in the house and did the dishes, feeling virtuous for not leaving them, and then Alice and I got our beds set up in the boat. There was just enough space for the two of us to squeeze in side by side. We took all the lounge chair cushions Milo hadn't used and added them to the hammock cushions when we gathered our bedding. Milo helped us put the cover on the boat to close us in for the night, though we planned to leave it unrolled a little at the bottom.

"It would break the camping mood to just go inside until bedtime," Alice said when we finished, and she ran back over to the blanket next to Milo's tent. He was already there, playing games on his iPod. "Tell me a bedtime story," she said, looking up at him in a way that even Milo now and then finds irresistible.

"Okay," Milo said. "I'll be done with this game in a minute and I'll do that."

Alice waited quietly for a few minutes before asking, "Aren't you finished yet?"

"Almost," Milo said. "I'm very good at this game."

A few more moments passed. It was completely quiet except for the little slap of the current against the dock and chattering from the birds as they too got ready for the night.

"Milo..." Alice said, in the sort of reminding voice that lets you know her patience won't last much longer. "Have you forgotten about my story?" He put down his iPod.

"Well, okay," Milo began. "Once upon a time there lived an owl family. They were a really great family. There was a father, mother, and about three little owl children. They had a family business making computer games."

"That does not sound possible at all," Alice objected. "I don't think owls care about stuff like that."

"You mean they don't give a hoot about it," I said. Alice laughed but Milo ignored me.

"If you're fine with books about a badger who runs

around in dresses, I don't see why you would object to a family of owls doing computer animation," Milo said. "Keep your standards consistent."

"All right, they can do whatever it is you said they do," Alice agreed. "Go on."

"The mother had to be away taking care of the grandparent owls, and the father had a lot of work to do with his business," Milo said. "One day they were all alone and had to fend for themselves. The father made sure they had plenty of dead mice to eat, with a few unlucky birds thrown in."

"Gross," Alice interjected.

"To you, maybe, but they thought it was all absolutely delicious. The father tucked them in securely for the day because of course owls are nocturnal. They're as afraid during the daytime as humans are at night. Daytime is much more dangerous for owls because they're sleeping. All the bad stuff happens during the day."

"Is this going to be a scary story?" Alice said suspiciously. "Because I'm not sure I want one of those."

"It's not too bad," Milo said. "As I was saying, the father got them all tucked in for the day. He remembered everything. Well, except for the snipes."

"Milo, this seems to be headed in the wrong direction," I said, but he shook his head.

"Our sister is a tougher kid than we were at her age," Milo said, slapping Alice on the back. "When we were six, we watched *Winnie the Pooh*. Alice watches *The Lord of the Rings* and lots of stuff that would have freaked us out, stuff that Mom and Dad would never have let us see at her age. We would have been terrified by the story I'm about to tell because we were sheltered babies, but Alice here won't be bothered by just a little violence, will you, Alice?"

"Of course not," Alice said, obviously liking the

elevated status Milo gave her. She snuggled up next to him. "I'm getting a little nervous, though, about what the owl father forgot. It wouldn't be something that *our* father forgot, would it?"

"Oh, I don't think so," Milo replied. "Because there aren't snipes around here. At least, I don't think there are."

"Milo!" I said warningly, but he only laughed.

"Oh, the Netherlands guidebook doesn't warn about snipes, so we're probably safe enough here. I wish I could say the same about our little owl friends. The snipes were birds of terror that circled the nests of poor baby owls, swooping down with no warning to peck their eyes out."

Alice screamed and dived for my lap. "Great job, Milo," I snapped. "You don't have to sleep in the same boat with her tonight. Let's go to bed, Alice. I'll tell you a better story once we get there."

"But I have to know what happens," Alice begged. "Are the baby owls going to be all right? Will the snipes get them and peck out their eyes?" She clutched my arm. "Charlotte, what if Milo is wrong and there are snipes around here, and they get in the boat tonight? Can we put the cover all the way down? And then lock it somehow?"

I glared at Milo. "I am totally going to get you for this," I hissed. He just snickered and went back to his iPod. I led Alice into the house to go to the bathroom one last time before Milo locked the house. While we were inside, I grabbed a twist tie from the bread loaf on the counter and stuffed it in my pocket.

Milo was already in the tent when we came out. As we passed it, he made muffled hooting noises. Alice squealed again and wriggled into the boat so fast I had a hard time holding it still.

"I'll be back in a minute," I whispered to Alice. "There's one more thing I have to do before we go to sleep."

I sat on the dock until I heard Milo zipping up his tent, and then I crawled over to it. Sure enough, he hadn't zipped it quite all the way down. There was just enough light left that I could see where the zipper pieces met, and as silently as I could, I used the twist tie to thread them together so they wouldn't open when he tried to get out. I was surprised Milo didn't notice what I was doing, but I could hear faint music coming from his iPod and guessed he had his earphones in.

I crept away, satisfied. There. That would give him just a little bit of irritation to make up for the trouble I was going to have trying to get Alice to sleep tonight. I tiptoed back to the boat and climbed underneath the cover.

"I'm glad you're back," Alice whispered. "It's a little scary in alone, especially if you're worried there might be snipes around."

"Those baby owls from Milo's story are fine," I said. "He was wrong about everything in their lives. They actually have a yarn business. They knit hats and scarves in all different colors, so their nests look like rainbows in the trees, and everything is very soft for the baby owls. The owl parents are too busy to leave the trees since the business is so successful. There aren't any snipes around, and all three baby owls grow up in peace and harmony."

"Milo's story sounded more real than yours does," Alice said. "No offense or anything, Charlotte."

"None taken," I said. "Well, since you didn't like that, how about if we just recite as much of *Bedtime for Frances* as we can remember and see if that puts you to sleep?"

"Good idea," Alice said, and she began. "'The big hand of the clock was at twelve. The little hand was at seven. It was seven o'clock. It was time for bed.'"

We recited lines back and forth until neither of us

could remember any more, but by then the rocking motion of the boat seemed to have done its work, and Alice stopped talking. I lay next to her quietly, loving the feeling of the boat on the water. Except for the musty smell from the cover, the rowboat made a perfect cocoon. The crickets and frogs nearby sounded companionable, but they weren't too close.

I was just drifting off to sleep when I heard what sounded like the zipper from the tent being worked vigorously up and down, followed by a few muffled, angry words from Milo. I giggled. It served him right. Finally there was a snapping noise, the sound of the zipper going all the way up, and then an exasperated huff as Milo stomped out of the tent, and then the sound of the back door opening and closing.

I snuggled down into the comforter and let myself daydream about an ocean voyage on a luxury liner. My maid unpacked a trunk full of beautiful clothes while I explored the ship. When I went to sleep, my unconscious mind just took the story over. It was winter, it must have been, because in my dream the ship hit an iceberg. We hit it so hard that the boat smashed apart, sending me flying through the air and into the ocean. The icy cold of the water shocked me awake and asleep at the same time, but when I saw Alice come up crying and gasping for air, I knew this wasn't a dream.

11

In Deep

I grabbed Alice's pajama shirt and pulled her up high enough to get her head above water. She took a breath and tried to scream, and she wrapped one arm around my neck so tightly I couldn't move my arms. We both went under.

The frigid water numbed everything, including my brain. I willed myself not to breathe, but everything in my body screamed for air. I fought Alice's hand. My feet touched the bottom, but I flailed in the water and managed to push my way back up again. Higher, higher...just enough to get my eyes and nose above the surface. I could hear the motor of a boat close by and people shouting, and saw a life ring hit the water next to me. I snatched it with one hand. Alice had gone limp, and I tried desperately to hold on to her with the other one, but she was so heavy and I was so cold.

I spit out a mouth full of water. "I can't get her up!" I shouted. Or at least, I tried to. I don't know if any words actually came out.

The motorboat circled us, but that only churned the waves up higher and pushed us back down. I came up again, gasping as I clung to the ring. A rowboat was coming closer than the motorboat could. Time slowed down and it seemed like hours but was probably only moments before I saw that it was Mr. de Hooch rowing toward us. He leaned out, and I pushed Alice up with everything I had. Somehow he got her from me and pulled her into the rowboat. As he turned her over on his lap she sort of gurgled and spat out a lot of water. She started to cry, which I thought was a good sign, but her left arm hung down in a peculiar way.

"Can you keep holding the ring and swim to the dock over here?" Mr. de Hooch shouted to me. "I'm afraid to risk upsetting the boat by pulling you in."

My teeth chattered as I nodded. I knew where we were now—just down from their house, where the main canal joined ours. I could see our own rowboat, split into two pieces, sinking down under the water in the early morning light. The cushions and pillows floated on the surface. I couldn't comprehend it. How had it happened? The boat had been safely tied on both ends when I climbed in last night.

Mr. de Hooch was shouting in Dutch at the two teenage boys in the motorboat, and they both looked terrified by the anger in his voice. Slowly, they followed the rowboat to the dock.

Milo crashed through the reeds and toward the dock just then, looking more frightened than I've ever seen him look in my life. Mrs. de Hooch was hurrying down the path from their house. Mr. de Hooch tossed the tow rope to Milo just as he reached the dock. "Tie us in," he shouted. "As tight as you can. And Jacoba," he called to his wife, "we need blankets, and hurry!" The next moment Milo had the rope and was pulling us in as hard and as fast as he could.

"I've got to pass the little girl up to you," Mr. de Hooch told Milo, breathing hard. "With my bad leg I can't stand up and hold her too. Be careful of her arm."

Milo snatched Alice from him and held her tight, staggering under her weight as he stood up. I thought he would start shouting at me and asking what on earth we'd done to make this happen, but he didn't. He looked like he was going to throw up. And suddenly, I knew.

"Our rowboat is all broken," Alice sobbed to Milo. "How did it get broken? I was having so much fun." She seemed too worried about the broken boat to notice that her arm was broken too, or maybe because of the shock she didn't care.

"It was my fault," Milo choked out. "It was all my fault. I'm so sorry, Alice. I'm so sorry."

"There's no time for any of that now," Mr. de Hooch said, breathing hard as he tied the rope to the ring on the dock. "You can talk it all out later. We need to get to the hospital."

He heaved himself out of the boat onto the dock at the same time Mrs. de Hooch appeared, hurrying back down the path with an armful of blankets. I shivered uncontrollably and cold water dripped off my clothes. Mrs. de Hooch shook out a blanket and tucked it around Alice, and then she wrapped one around me. It was made of fine, soft wool and smelled like lavender. I shuddered, pulling the blanket tighter around my shoulders as I watched Mr. de Hooch checking Alice over.

"I had some first aid training in the army," he said to Milo and me. "And she looks better than I thought she would, though this arm is definitely broken. I think I can drive her to the hospital in Steenwijk faster than an ambulance could get here. Her breathing is fine now, that's the main thing, and the arm looks like a simple fracture. Let's carry her to my car, and we'll drive down and pick up your parents."

Milo and I looked at each other, scared. Would Dad get in trouble for leaving us alone? Milo cleared his throat. "Dad's not here, sir," he said. "He stayed in Amsterdam last night."

Mr. and Mrs. de Hooch exchanged looks of their own.

"He'll need to be notified," Mr. de Hooch said, after a silent pause. "Can we call him?"

"The phone with his number is in my pocket," Milo said. "I'd have to put Alice down to call."

"Carry her to the car first," Mr. de Hooch directed. "I wish I could carry her myself. Cursed leg. But anyway, now that we don't quite have an absolute emergency, there are a few more things I want to say to those boys over there." He pointed toward the motorboat, which was idling next to the dock.

"Come this way, to the car," Mrs. de Hooch said to Milo, and still holding Alice, he followed her down the path and to the driveway. His arms trembled from the weight of her and the heavy blanket. I stayed a moment more to see what Mr. de Hooch would do. The boys had struck our rowboat, that was clear, but I couldn't figure out how it had happened.

Mr. de Hooch didn't yell at them, but I didn't have to understand Dutch to know I wouldn't want him saying any of it to me. I couldn't understand the boys' response either, but I'm fairly sure there was a "yes, sir" equivalent in Dutch over and over from each of them. Mr. de Hooch swung back around to me.

"They're not bad kids," he said, as the motorboat pulled away and disappeared down the canal. "They were going much too fast and they admit it. I suspect they may have had too much alcohol last night as well. They just never expected a boat to be drifting here. They will turn themselves in to the police, and I have their names and the boat information in case they don't, so that's all we can do. Come on," he said to me, and put his arm around my shoulder and led me to the car. It felt good to let someone else be in charge.

Milo had just got Dad on the phone when we reached

the garage, and that's when I heard the whole story for the first time.

"Alice and Charlotte had an accident in the boat, Dad. Alice's arm is broken and she swallowed lots of water, but Mr. de Hooch thinks she's going to be OK. Charlotte is kind of shaken up but she's OK, too. It was my fault, Dad. All my fault." Milo looked up and saw us come into the garage, and he turned around for a moment so he didn't have to face me while he continued.

"We camped out last night, and they slept in the rowboat. I know, we shouldn't have done that without asking. We kind of pranked each other, and to get back at Charlotte I undid one of the ropes and let the other one out so the boat would drift a little way into the canal. I tied it really tight, though. I don't know how it broke away. The rope's probably really old, and I didn't think about that, so I don't know. Maybe it snapped or something. There was a lot of wind during the night. I didn't know how much there would be, or I would never have, never..." Milo stopped talking then. He was crying.

"I guess the rowboat drifted down and out to the mouth of the big canal. Some kids were out in a motor boat and didn't see it as they came around the curve, and smashed into them." He paused again. "I know, Dad, I know. It was beyond stupid, but I never meant to hurt either of them, I promise. I just didn't think. I can't believe I did something so dumb." He stopped to listen a little more and then handed the phone to Mr. de Hooch.

"Your girls are not seriously injured," Mr. de Hooch told Dad. "I'm taking them to the hospital in Steenwijk. We'll likely be done and out before you could get there, so just come to your house. I'll call you when I can." He paused a moment and said, "I want you to know your boy seems very contrite. It's obvious he cares for his sisters a great deal." He turned at looked at me. "And your bigger girl is heroic. She kept hold of the little one somehow without drowning both of them. I don't know how she did it, honestly. She doesn't look strong enough."

I thought I was so cold that nothing could warm me up, but suddenly I was warm all through. I felt like I might be able to do anything, and I wanted to be good for the rest of my life.

Dad must have thanked him because Mr. de Hooch said, "I'm glad we can help." He looked into the car to the backseat, where Mrs. de Hooch was holding a whimpering Alice on her lap. "I'm very glad we can help," he repeated, softer this time.

Mr. de Hooch told Milo to get in the front seat, and I slid in next to Mrs. de Hooch and Alice. Before I could close the door, Jaap hopped in and put his paws up on Mrs. de Hooch's lap, for all the world as though he wanted to check on Alice.

"Oh, please, can he come too?" Alice begged, reaching out to touch Jaap's silky ear with her good arm.

"You can't take a dog into a hospital, Alice," I said, but Mr. de Hooch just laughed as he got into the car.

"We can probably get away with it," he said. "You can stay, Jaap." The dog leaped up on the seat next to Alice, sniffed her all over, and she stopped crying and smiled.

We stopped at our house so I could put on dry clothes and get some for Alice, too, and then we drove to Steenwijk. It takes us over an hour to get there on our bikes, but in the de Hooch's car we arrived in about ten minutes.

Mr. de Hooch pulled the car outside the emergency entrance and parked. He went inside and in a moment returned with two orderlies. One took the keys to move the car and another had a wheelchair for Alice.

We followed behind as the orderly took her in. Hospital workers seemed to be watching for us, and we didn't have to wait at all. "Do you always get in this fast in Dutch hospitals?" Milo asked, confused.

The orderly laughed. He was about to say something when Mr. de Hooch interrupted him and told Milo, "They know who I am. They should, after three surgeries and a great deal of physical therapy."

"That's right," the orderly said, grinning. "And then there was that little thing you did in peacekeeping for the United Nations. That makes you stand out a little more." Then he said something else in Dutch that I didn't understand, and he and Mr. de Hooch both laughed.

The United Nations! So that explained it, explained everything. Mr. de Hooch had had an important job. That was why he always looked so immaculate and was so good with people. Evidently the de Hooches had retired to sleepy little Ossenzijl for peace and quiet after his long career. And Mrs. de Hooch just wanted privacy now that they could finally have it. I'd gotten the whole thing wrong. There was no mystery after all.

The orderly took us to a room so nice it barely looked like a hospital room, and we didn't have to wait even a few minutes before a doctor came to look at Alice and me. The doctor made us both lie down and a nurse brought in a stack of hot blankets, which she piled on top of us. Alice's arm, however, was covered in ice packs.

"Are you trying to warm me up or freeze me up?" Alice asked, her teeth chattering.

"I'm sorry, but we need to keep your arm from swelling," the nurse replied. "Would some hot chocolate help? And I'll bring some for you too," she said, turning to me. She was back in just a few minutes. I couldn't remember anything tasting so good in my whole life before.

The nurse brought tea for the others and some little shortbread biscuits, and suddenly I remembered this should be breakfast time on a normal day.

The doctor spoke to Mr. de Hooch in Dutch, and then they called Dad on the phone to let him know I was all right, and Alice's arm needed to be set. The nurse came back in and gave Alice a shot.

"It's to make you a little sleepy and relaxed while the doctor fixes your arm," she explained, when Alice frowned at the needle.

Jaap had curled up on the warm blankets next to Alice, on the opposite side from the ice packs. I couldn't believe no one said a word about a dog in the hospital, but the doctors and nurses just pretended he wasn't there. Alice kept her hand on the top of Jaap's head and stroked it. The little dog's tail thumped.

"It is the scratching under his left ear, that he really likes," Mrs. de Hooch told her, and sure enough, when Alice stroked him there Jaap pushed his nose even closer.

"He really seems to like you," Mr. de Hooch said, smiling.

"Someday I'm going to have a dog...like this," Alice began, but her voice sounded foggier and less distinct by the word. "And maybe...some cats...too." She wasn't sleeping, but wasn't exactly awake, either.

Without Alice's chattering, the room grew quiet, but it was a comfortable quiet. "Excuse me for prying," Mr. de Hooch finally said, turning to Milo and me. "But why have I never seen your mother? Did she come with you on this trip?"

In a few minutes I told them everything. How Dad and Mom had always wanted to bring us to Europe, and how Dad got the job in Amsterdam for the summer and then found the house online and rented it. And then I told her about Grandma Sybil getting cancer and how Mom went home to take care of her. I missed Mom so much right then I got a lump in my throat, and to keep from crying I changed the subject and told them about moving to Oregon as soon as we got back to the United States. They were very good listeners, and somewhere in the telling Mrs. de Hooch ended up patting my hand. She was every bit as nice as I'd somehow known she would be.

"The moving so often, this we understand very well," Mrs. de Hooch told me. "We have moved twenty-six times. It is a luxury to be able to stay in one place now and know that we will never move again."

"Yes," Mr. de Hooch said, "But it's not a bad thing to see the world when you're young and know how people live in many different places. When you are older, you will see how it gives you a broad perspective. You will understand people in a way that others do not."

"It isn't easy now, though," I said. "I hate it." The words came out with such force it shocked me.

"Oh no, not easy, now," Mrs. de Hooch agreed. "And not all good either. It was hard for our daughter, when she was growing up. Each time we moved, there were tears. We had to remind her that as long as we were happy together, we were home. And so are you, when your whole family is together. You three are lucky to have each other. Our daughter did not have that."

I thought about how Milo and I made each others' lives miserable more often than not. About the pointless arguments we had way too often, and how the seemingly silly things we had done last night just to annoy each other meant we'd almost lost Alice. For sure, none of that made me enjoy home more, wherever that happened to be. I glanced over at Milo. His eyes met mine for about a microsecond before we looked away, and I think he was probably thinking the same thing I was.

"Where is your daughter?" I asked them. "Does she live in Ossenzijl too? Is that why you came to live here?"

"No, she is a diplomat in Africa," Mr. de Hooch replied. "I'm afraid we don't get to see her nearly as often as we'd like."

"And that is one of the problems of the life we chose," Mrs. de Hooch said, sighing. "We lived everywhere else while she was growing up, and now she thinks it's normal to live far away from home."

"Do you go see her?" I asked, and Mr. de Hooch hesitated.

"It's a bit of a bother for her to have us because of my former career. So she comes and visits us when she can, and we talk to her on the telephone and Skype too. You are part of the computer generation, so you probably know all about that," he said, smiling.

The doctor came back in. "It's time to see about that arm," he said, and in about thirty seconds he had straightened Alice's arm out so it looked normal again. She made a little squeak, which made Jaap growl low in his throat, but the whole thing was over fast. Alice barely seemed to care afterwards, though Jaap jumped off the bed and stared up at the doctor with distrustful eyes. The same nurse who'd brought us the hot chocolate wrapped Alice's arm in a bright blue cast.

"Pretty," Alice murmured, and sort of dozed off again.

Milo's eyes were glued to Alice. He chewed on his bottom lip, his face tense and miserable. Later, when we were alone at the house, I would tell him I understood and that I didn't blame him for anything that had happened. It was as much my fault as his.

I was so tired by then I barely remember leaving the

hospital or the drive home in the de Hooch's car, but Alice seemed to be perking up. When we arrived at home, Dad was waiting at the bench at the end of the driveway, and as soon as he opened the car door, she held out her cast. "They said it's Dutch blue," she bragged. "And it's OK for me to have that color, even if I'm an American because I'm a special visitor. The nurse said I kind of got baptized into a Dutch person in our canal!"

Dad picked up Alice and held her tight. "You gave me a terrible scare, Miss Alice," he said, and his voice wobbled a little bit as he kissed her head. "I'm so thankful you're all right." Mr. de Hooch got out of the car and he came over to shake Dad's hand.

"Your name is Jeremy, your children tell me," he said. "I'm Pieter de Hooch."

"He worked for the United Nations, Dad!" I blurted. I couldn't wait to tell Dad about our royal treatment at the hospital, but I wouldn't do that until after they left.

"Mr. de Hooch," Dad began, but Mr. de Hooch stopped him.

"I'm just Pieter to my friends, and my wife is Jacoba." Dad shifted Alice to reach into the car and shake her hand too.

"I am sorry you and I had to meet under these circumstances," Mr. de Hooch said. "You have three delightful children."

"You must think they have terrible, neglectful parents," Dad said. "I don't know what I was thinking, leaving them overnight like that. I should have known better. My wife is the one who worries, and I usually leave that to her. Since she's not here, I should have done a better job of doing the worrying for her. Alice and Charlotte could have been killed."

"Accidents can happen when parents are at home,

too," Mr. de Hooch reminded him. "These children's guardian angels seem to have stepped in for you."

"Some guardian angel neighbors did too," Dad said. "Don't think I don't understand that. I'm very grateful for everything you did for them today."

"I know you are," Mr. de Hooch said. "I'm a father myself. There's no need to say another word about it."

As I got out of the car, Mrs. de Hooch squeezed my hand. "I hope you will come down and visit to let me know how you're getting along," she said. "As soon as you're feeling up to it."

"I'd love to," I said. "Thank you for everything. And you too, sir," I said.

"I've had enough of sir for my lifetime," he said, and his eyes crinkled.

"They seem like wonderful people," Dad said, as the de Hooch's Mercedes drove slowly down the street toward their house. Without putting Alice down, he hugged me with his other arm.

"The best," I said, hugging him back.

"And their dog is just as good as they are," Alice added, and we all laughed, at least, all of us but Milo.

12

Aftermath

Dad fixed us a late breakfast of eggs and toast. I ate every bite and so did Alice. Milo only pushed the food around on his plate, and after a few minutes of pretending to eat, he went outside. Through the window I could see him crouched down at the dock, examining the rope.

"It was completely frayed at the broken point," Dad said, looking out at Milo too. "I checked it myself before you got back. He couldn't have seen that in the dark last night, and anyway, the rope was mostly underwater. I hope he can forgive himself. I understand how hard that would be, though."

He gave me a tight little smile. "I'm not looking forward to what may just be the worst conversation of my life, the one where we have to tell your mother what happened. It's a good thing we're on separate continents because she'll want to wring my neck. Then she'll either want to get on a plane immediately, or have all of you on a plane immediately, and I don't see how either option is possible right now. I also don't see how I can convince her of that."

For a minute I hoped he wouldn't be able to. I missed Mom so much today. "I wish she could come back," I said. I couldn't say anything else.

"Me too," Dad admitted. "Grandma Sybil's getting better. The treatment she's getting is just a precaution, but it's rough and she still needs Mom more than we do.

Knowing she's needed there doesn't make it any easier for us, though."

It seemed like I'd just heard that somewhere else, and I thought about Mr. and Mrs. de Hooch and our conversation about moving around so much. It seems like everybody has something they have to do that's just hard. Grandma Sybil's cancer is hard, and Mom's being gone is too. Moving to Oregon will be hard and so will the move after that. Someday, after I've grown up, I'm going to find my own home like the de Hooches did, and I'll never move again. But then there will be other hard things to get through. That's just how life is.

That thought should have depressed me, but somehow it didn't. God would take care of it. He was helping me do the hard things, one after another, and even enjoy the good times in between. The accident this morning had been a hard thing, but it was mostly over now and things would get better soon. I took my dishes to the sink.

"Forget about those, I'll do them," Dad said, as I started to fill the sink with soapy water. "You've earned a rest for sure." He looked over to the couch, where Alice had fallen fast asleep thanks to her pain medication. "I'd say rescuing your sister ought to be good for a day off chores."

"I'm not a hero, Dad," I said. "There wasn't time to think. I just had to get her out, so somehow I did. With a lot of help from Mr. de Hooch," I added. "And God too, I think."

Dad smiled. "Not everybody knows at your age what they're really made of, Charlotte. Let's just say I'm very proud of you."

Suddenly I was so tired I knew I couldn't stay awake another minute. I went upstairs to bed and the rest of the day was more or less a blur. Dad must have moved Alice to our room because later I woke up to hear her sobbing, and for a minute I thought the accident had happened all over again. I sat up, but I saw that Mrs. de Hooch was already there, holding Alice up to take some medicine and soothing her back down again when she continued to cry. Seeing her there so unexpectedly startled me all the way awake. I wondered how long she'd been at our house.

"My arm hurts again, really bad," Alice wept. "And I want Mommy. I want her here right now."

I wanted her too, and as soon as Alice said so out loud the reality of the accident hit me again—how scary it had been, and how I might not have been able to get out of the canal with Alice if Mr. de Hooch hadn't happened to be up so early to see it all happen. I turned over and cried as silently as I could. A few minutes later, I heard Alice snoring. I guess the medicine must have knocked her right back out.

The floor creaked as Mrs. de Hooch got up, and though my eyes were squeezed shut to try to stop the tears from coming, I could hear her moving quietly around the room, neatening things up, smoothing the bedding, and opening the window. I liked having her there, taking care of us like Mom would have. She started to leave the room, hesitated, and came back in and stood beside me. I opened my eyes and looked up at her.

"Is there anything that you need, Charlotte?" she asked. "Anything I can help with, anything at all?"

I didn't answer. I couldn't because the tears started up again. Mrs. de Hooch didn't say anything but sat right down on the bed and squeezed my shoulder. "It's all turned out all right," she said, and her calm voice made me believe it. "Rest some more. You are fine, and Alice will be too." She left the room and went downstairs.

I woke up at suppertime. Alice and Milo were already

at the table eating soup with Dad. Alice was still a little loopy from the medicine, and seemed perplexed about how to get her spoon from her bowl up to her mouth. It would have been funny to watch if I hadn't known how close she'd just come to drowning. Dad helped her.

"Have a seat," he said. "Mrs. de Hooch kindly brought over a big pot of some delicious-looking split pea and ham soup when she checked on you two earlier, but I'm going to wait to eat until we're done calling your mother. Just thinking about making that call makes my stomach churn."

Dad was right. Mom nearly had a heart attack when she found out what happened.

"This is some kind of sick joke, right?" she demanded, after Dad gave her a quick version of the accident. When Alice waved her cast proudly in front of the screen, Mom closed her eyes, and when she opened them again and the cast was still there, she shook her head.

"I can't believe all this," she said flatly. "Jeremy, this plan isn't working. I think we need to figure out a way to all be back together again. You're only going in to the office every other week. Can't you just do the work from here? Or maybe you should quit. Surely they would understand why. I want all three of my children still alive at the end of the summer."

I thought Dad would start apologizing, but he surprised me.

"No, Meg," he said. "This was a crazy accident. Even if you'd been here and I'd been here, we might have let the kids sleep outside, and the same thing could have happened. We might have been closer to the accident, but that probably wouldn't have prevented it."

Mom put her hand to her head as though she had a headache coming on. "That's true," she admitted. "But I can't forgive myself for not being there today. If the worst had happened, and it almost did…" Her lips trembled. "Mama's still not well enough that I can feel good about her being here alone. But maybe now she could go to Jack and Tracy's. If she'd agree to it."

"No," Dad said. "We had a good reason for deciding the kids and I would stay here, and there's a good reason why you're there in Kansas City with your mother. We prayed about it then; I've prayed about it now—believe me, I've prayed about it now, Meg—and I think it's still the right thing. Obviously I won't ever leave the kids here alone to go into the office again, and that's a promise. But other than that, we're all going to keep on doing the best we can. The summer's almost half over. We can do this. And we will."

It sounded like a battle speech, and in a way I guess it was.

"But Alice will need…" Mom began.

"Alice is going to be just fine," Dad said. "After today, I don't think the cast even will slow her down much."

"All right," Mom said, defeated. "I don't like it, but hopefully this is the worst that's going to happen."

"It better be," Dad said fervently.

We changed the subject, and she told us about last night's dinner with Uncle Jack and Aunt Tracy, Annabeth and Anthony. "Annabeth said to make sure to tell you to keep up with the journal," Mom told me. "Actually, she said she'd murder you if you didn't, but I'm sure she meant that metaphorically. Will you let me see any of it later?"

I had plenty of material for my next entry, that's for sure. "Some of it you can see," I said. I wasn't sure how much I wanted to share.

We talked a little more and then Dad shooed us away

from the computer. I went upstairs to choose my clothes for tomorrow, but I could still hear the two of them talking, though they lowered their voices. I'm not sure if they were arguing or not, but they both sounded like they had their minds made up about something.

When they finished, Dad called us downstairs for another meeting, and this one was much different than the one two nights ago.

"All right," he said. "I put up a good front for Mom's benefit, but don't think you're off the hook with me. Things are definitely going to change. How about you tell me what some of those changes will be."

"No more pranking," I said.

"Right," Dad said. "It's poisoning the atmosphere around here. Keep going."

"No more dumb arguments," Milo said, barely looking up.

"Right again," Dad said. "Somehow I think you'll be less tempted by those than in the past. What happened today was a hard lesson but perhaps a valuable one. Anything else?"

We couldn't think of anything, but Dad was just warming up, and I braced myself. "You need work, meaningful work," he said. "Especially you two older kids. I'm all for summer vacation, but we're not at home, and there are too many hours to fill in a strange place, and only one parent to make sure you're spending them well. I am that parent, and unfortunately, I need to spend some of my time making a living. I'm upping everyone's chores. And school is back in session." We groaned.

"Remember all those books your mother brought along from Boston for you to read during this trip?" Dad reminded us. "The ones still in a stack by her side of the bed? Take those to your rooms and start reading them. And that's not the only schoolwork I want you to do. I'm giving you a big assignment."

"You want me to complete the Boy Scout canoeing badge?" Milo asked, looking up for the first time.

"Sure, why not?" Dad agreed. "But that's not my assignment, so canoe on your own time. You're going to write a book." We stared at him.

Milo recovered first. "What?" he demanded. "Come on, Dad, that's the kind of half-baked idea parents get sometimes and then drop in a couple days when they realize it's not a workable plan."

"I don't appreciate your tone of voice or your implication," Dad said, pounding the table. "It *is* a workable plan, and you will not be dropping it. We're doing this for Mom, who is understandably distressed about the careless way you've been spending your free time. If this had happened while she was here, you know as well as I do that your school vacation would be over. Abruptly. Completely. Finally. And it is."

"No, Daddy!" Alice cried. "It's probably illegal to do schoolwork in the summer!"

Dad ignored her. "You three will meet together and write for a minimum of an hour daily for the remainder of our time here. Then you will also have two independent research periods throughout the day. During this process you will work together, you will each have a theme, and you will find some way to tie those themes together."

"What kind of themes?" I asked, suspiciously. Alice wrinkled her eyebrows. I don't think she had any idea what he was talking about.

"I have to make it fun for me, too," he said. "So you'll be writing about Dutch art. Maybe you can use your mother's books as a starting point. I've got to go back in to Amsterdam day after tomorrow. Hopefully you girls will be up to a trip by then. While we're there we'll go back to the museum. Each of you can pick your own favorite painting, and make it a good choice because it will become your book topic. And then somehow you will also find a way to work your story around the other two choices."

"Daddy," Alice said. "Does our art theme have to be a painting?"

"It doesn't need to be a painting, but it needs to be a work of art," Dad replied. "There are plenty of statues or other kinds of art in the Rijksmuseum, Alice. Lots to choose from."

"My favorite art isn't in the museum," Alice said. "It's the lizard garden. I want to think about that."

Dad thought for a minute. "It doesn't have to be from the museum. The lizards are Dutch art too. They could be a fine choice."

"Alice can't write a book with us," I said. "She can barely write anything."

"I can too," Alice started to say, but Milo stopped her.

"I guess we can help you," he said, and Dad put his hand on Milo's shoulder as Alice looked at him in surprise.

"Good catch, son," he said. "Good catch."

That night I couldn't sleep. Each time I dozed off, I jerked awake thinking I was back in the water. I could feel the horror of being sucked down into mud at the bottom that felt like wet cement. I kept reliving the one terrified moment when I'd been sure I'd never get back to the surface again with Alice. When the flashback happened a third time, I finally got up. In the bed across from mine, Alice slept peacefully, her casted arm resting on a pillow. Thank goodness for the extras in the linen closet since the pillows that used to be on our beds were probably waterlogged in canal mud by now.

I went to the window and looked out. It was just

twilight outside, and in the half dark I saw the place where the rowboat had always been. The view without it was like seeing Alice's smile with a new tooth missing, and my eyes couldn't stay away from the empty spot. Dad would have to pay the owners the cost of the boat, and now we could only go out in the canoe. Alice probably couldn't do that at all, since if it tipped over, she would drench her cast. I didn't need a cast to keep me away from the water. When I thought about going out in a boat again myself, any boat, cold sweat broke out on my neck.

I went downstairs to get a drink. Dad sat at the desk working on the computer. "Can't sleep?" he asked me sympathetically. I shook my head.

"No," I said. I felt like a baby asking, but found myself doing it anyway. "Do you think we could try calling Mom again? I'd just like to talk to her. Would she be home or still at the hospital with Grandma Sybil?"

"There's one way to find out," Dad said, pulling up Skype on his laptop. A moment later the computer produced a gurgling noise followed by a sound like a phone ringing. "All set," he said. "Do you want to talk to her alone?"

"If you don't mind," I said.

"I'll leave you to it then," he said, and went to his bedroom across from the kitchen and closed the door behind him.

The computer gurgled again and I knew Mom had heard it ring and was signing on. But then there was the sound of random keys being hit and a cross voice muttered, "I wonder how you get this fool thing to work?"

"You just did," I said, giggling. It felt so good to laugh. "Hi, Grandma Sybil. How are you?"

"Alive and kicking," she replied. "Madder than you know what about these so-called treatments, but what can you do? Just a few more weeks and I'm through with all of it. But congratulations. I understand you're alive and did plenty of kicking yourself this morning."

"I guess you could put it that way," I said.

"Your mother's worried sick about you kids, but any granddaughter of mine worth her salt would never give up and have a permanent tea party at the bottom of the canal with her little sister," Grandma Sybil said. "You don't have it in you to get yourself killed at the age of twelve, and I can see that, even if your own mother doesn't. I refuse to worry about you."

A little of the warm glow I'd felt earlier when Mr. de Hooch praised me on the phone to Dad came back. "Thanks," I said. "I wasn't sure at the time it would work out that way."

"You underestimate yourself," Grandma Sybil said. "Not that it wasn't a ghastly thing to go through, I'm sure. How are you holding up?"

"Not so great," I confessed. "That's why I called."

"Well, your mother is at the pharmacy picking up some bottled torture for me to swallow," Grandma Sybil said. "I wish she were here instead, so she could talk to you."

"Maybe I need someone to tell me to get over it," I said, "and you always do a good job of that."

"I've had years of practice with that kind of thing for sure," Grandma Sybil agreed, "even if I'm not sure that's what you need right now. Charlotte, Meg is always telling me she can look at you all when she talks on the computer, but I don't see a thing. It just sounds like a bad phone call. I've got something to show you. Maybe it will give you a laugh."

"Hit the little button with the camera," I said, and a minute later I could see Grandma Sybil peering into the screen. "Hey, it worked," she said in surprise.

But was that Grandma Sybil? She'd always worn her hair in a really short, straight, no-nonsense haircut. Now she had longer, loosely-curled hair. I couldn't believe how good it looked on her.

"Grandma Sybil, I love it!" I exclaimed.

She looked pleased. "I just got this wig today. I couldn't decide whether I liked it or if I was making a fool of myself. I'm glad you approve."

"No, keep it, it looks great," I said. "You don't look like I'm used to seeing you, but...."

"But it's better than my real hair," Grandma Sybil supplied. "Go on, just say so. I know it's true. I've always had thin, straight hair that couldn't hold a curl worth beans, but of course, it all fell out from the chemo. I can't say it was any great loss, although I'd rather have my own hair than be bald as an egg like I am underneath this wig." She patted her head to make sure her new hair was still in place.

"I've always secretly wondered what it would be like to wear my hair like this. It seemed like a wasted experience not to try it, when I could pick anything in the room. I thought your mom would fall off her chair when I chose this wig, but I couldn't resist."

"You look really pretty," I told her, and it was true. "You need some dangly earrings, and maybe a scarf. Tell Annabeth to find those for you. She's good at that sort of thing. And makeup. You should definitely try wearing makeup."

"Oh, go on now. I'm not sure I'm up for too much fancying up all at once," she said, touching her new hair. "None of my friends will even recognize me."

"Well, they can just get used to the new you, Grandma Sybil," I said. "I'm serious about the earrings."

"I'll think about it," she said, considering. "Charlotte,

I'd better go. Your mom rules me with an iron fist and it's time for my nap. If she gets home and finds me out of bed, she'll skin me alive."

This was an outrageous lie, and we both knew it. Grandma Sybil does whatever she wants. It was just her way of telling me she was too tired to talk anymore.

"Have a good nap," I said. "Thanks for talking to me. I feel better now."

"Thanks for not drowning earlier today," Grandma Sybil replied. "You have a good sleep too, and make yourself think about something pleasant as you're drifting off. It helps. That's what I always do. Don't think of big, exciting things, just small, nice ones. Like remembering the birds chattering or how good grass smells when you mow it the first time in the spring. Goodbye, honey."

The screen went black and I think she probably just closed Mom's laptop instead of logging off. I clicked out of Skype and got up from the computer.

"Goodnight, Dad," I called. "I'm done with your computer."

I went back to bed and tried to take Grandma Sybil's advice. I still couldn't stop thinking about today, but there had been good things too, and now I made myself think about those. I had two new real friends—well, three, if you counted Jaap. I closed my eyes. I remembered the smell of lavender from Mrs. de Hooch's blanket. I went to sleep, and this time I slept all night.

13

Night Watch and the Golden Girl

A few days later, we went to Amsterdam for Dad's meeting. When I woke up and heard the rain rattling against the windows that morning, I wished I could pull the covers over my head and stay in bed instead. We knew from experience that once we'd been out in weather like this for even a few minutes, we would be completely soaked afterwards, possibly for the whole day. After breakfast, Dad wrapped Alice's cast in a plastic garbage bag so it would stay dry.

We were on our way out the door when Dad put up his hand. "Notebook check," he said. "Have you got them?"

We looked at him blankly. "You're authors now, remember?" he reminded us. "Thus, you need notebooks for the copious amounts of notes you will each be taking at the Rijksmuseum and Lizard Square today."

"Real authors take notes on computers now," Milo said. "And they do their writing on them as well. Either we're going to be using your computer all the time, or we'll need to make a stop at the Apple store and pick up a laptop for each one of us."

"I love that idea," I said, grinning at Milo. "I'm positive notebooks for authors are obsolete."

"You will be writers in the tradition of Mark Twain, Charles Dickens, and Shakespeare himself," Dad replied. "Get your notebooks and pens."

Milo sighed. "Well, it was worth a try," he said. We went up to our rooms to get the notebooks that Mom, our always-prepared homeschool teacher, had packed for us. We hadn't touched them since she left.

"Grab an extra set of clothes in case we can't get back tonight or you get too wet," Dad called up to us. "If you girls get soaked, we don't need to add pneumonia to the fallout from the boat accident. Roll the stuff up as small as you can. I'll put it in my bag."

We were drenched from head to foot by the time we finally got to the train and found seats in Dad's favorite quiet car, where you're not supposed to speak above a whisper. I think he likes to sit here so he doesn't have to entertain us, but really, I like it too. I had my journal, wrapped up in another one of the plastic garbage bags from the house to keep it dry, and I wrote down everything I could remember about the accident while Alice played games on Dad's cell phone. When the train pulled into Amsterdam's Centraal Station, I still hadn't finished writing, but I carefully re-wrapped my notebook and we got off.

"My meeting's at eleven," Dad told us as we jostled through the crowds outside the station. "So we'll head over to the museum for an hour first, take a quick look through the park to see how Alice's lizards like the rain, and go on to the office from there."

"It took us forty-five minutes to walk to the museum the last time we were here," Milo pointed out, "and it's almost nine-thirty."

"Ah, but since you're part of the eager working class now, rather than mere idle children, we're taking the bus," Dad said. "That way we will be there in about five minutes." That news put us in a good mood, although in the morning thunderstorm, Amsterdam looked gloomier and dirtier than I remembered it being before.

We got off the bus across the street from the museum. Rain had turned the slate turrets on the roof a shiny black, and Alice couldn't resist stomping through puddles on the brick walkways, getting us even wetter than we already were until Dad made her stop. As we walked down the path toward the museum entrance, I looked over and saw the bench where a month ago, Mom got the texts that turned our whole vacation upside down. It was empty now, and it was easy to remember that day. Dad glanced at the bench too, and I knew he was thinking about it too. We went inside.

"Ready, set, go," Dad told Milo and me after he paid our admission. "You lead, and Alice and I'll follow. Choose wisely, kids, because you'll be spending a lot of time with these pieces, whatever they are."

I didn't need to go all over the museum to know which picture I wanted for my theme. I would choose my favorite, the one in the postcard Dad brought home by the other Pieter de Hooch. I had first seen the painting right in the middle of a fight with Milo. I thought maybe that was fitting, since this project is sort of a punishment for us not being able to get along. But I still liked it, and I led the rest of the family straight to the room with the dollhouse and my picture.

"I don't know," Milo said, once we got to the gallery and stood looking up at it. "If we have to write a whole book about just three things, don't you think you should choose something with more action? There's just one story here, the girl and her mother."

"Yes, but anything could be happening," I argued. "We don't know why the mother gives the jug to the little girl. Maybe it's worth a lot of money. Maybe it has a secret message inside, and the Dutch win an entire war when the little girl carries it to her father, who's a general in the army."

"I like this picture," Alice said. "I think the girl should be the hero of the book."

"Come on," Milo said in disgust. "I don't want to write a book with a little girl for a hero. It can't just be a girl's book. It has to work for all three of us."

"Dad said we could each have our own theme," I argued. "And somehow, we have to make it work for everyone else. That means you can choose whatever you want, and Alice and I make it work for us. And somehow, what I want goes into the story, too. The girl doesn't have to be the hero. She just has to be a big part of it somehow. What are you picking anyway?"

"Something completely different from yours," Milo replied. "The biggest picture in this place, and one that has plenty of action. Come on, I'll show you."

I was pretty sure I knew which one that would be, and sure enough we followed him up the marble staircase and through a walkway to where Rembrandt's *Night Watch* hung in its own gallery.

We'd all seen it a month ago, of course. It's the most famous painting in the museum and takes up a whole wall. That first time we came, the size of the picture was what caught my attention, along with the meticulous detail on the fine gold clothes of the man in the front. The painting is mostly dark, and his clothes made him stand out from all the other people in the painting. But this time, I needed to look for a story. We stood in front of it silently for a couple of minutes.

"What is your girl doing in this painting, Charlotte?" Alice finally asked, pointing. "Because there she is again. Why do you think she left her mother and came to a meeting with all of these men?"

Startled, I followed her finger. So did Milo, and he

laughed out loud. "Hey! It really could be the same kid. If she's a kid. It's kind of hard to tell. Maybe she's a dwarf adult. But she's got the exact same hair. We'll say it's the same girl. That is totally cool. Maybe this is going to work after all."

"The poor thing seems a little nervous," Alice said.

"I bet she's excited to be where something's happening instead of inside her dull, bare house," Milo said.

"Her house isn't dull," I objected. "I think it's beautiful. No, I don't think she's scared. Look at her face. She's listening. She's just overheard something really important, something that changes everything. Those men aren't paying any attention to her, and they don't even know she heard what they said. That makes her a perfect spy."

"Her dog came too," Alice commented, looking up at an outline hiding in the shadows. "You can barely see him, but I think he should be Jaap's grandfather or something. You can't see that he's a beautiful dog, but of course he must be, if he was Jaap's grandfather. He's listening too. He can be a spy dog."

"We should be taking notes," I said. "We should write down how many people are in this painting. That kind of thing."

Milo shook his head. "Those things aren't that important. We can buy posters of both paintings, and hang them up at the house and figure all that out. What we need to pay attention to, right now, are the smaller things in the background that we wouldn't see except on a canvas this big. I'm going to take pictures of it from every angle just in case we miss something." He took out his camera and meticulously took photo after photo, close ups of every area so we could blow them up on the computer at home. It was good thinking, and I was impressed.

"I wish I could see what's not in the picture," Alice said suddenly. "They're pointing at us just like we're pointing at them. Something's going on, right where we're standing. I wonder what it is." She turned around and looked behind us, hoping for a clue, but of course there wasn't one, just a number of other real people who wanted to look at the painting too. Dad was on the other side of the room, reading the displays about *The Night Watch*. He didn't seem to be paying any attention to us, but I realized we'd been standing right in the best spot for much too long. "Come on," I said. "We're being pigs." Reluctantly, we went over to join Dad.

"I don't suppose you'd buy us some posters?" I asked him. "For research purposes?"

"That sounds reasonable," he agreed.

"I still think laptops are essential for this project," Milo said.

"Laptops are unnecessary," Dad replied. "Completely unnecessary. But posters are in a different category. Let's make the shop visit quick, though. I need to get to my meeting."

"But my lizards!" Alice protested. "We can't forget them!"

"Don't worry, we won't," Dad assured her. "It's too late to see them now, but we'll eat lunch in the park after the meeting. I promise."

"If the rain has stopped, you could leave us there during the meeting," Milo suggested. "It'd be a lot more fun for us than sitting in an empty office waiting for you."

"You may think I learned nothing from our experience the other day, but you'd be wrong," Dad said. "There isn't a chance in the whole world I'd let you roam free in a crowded section of Amsterdam while I'm in a meeting. I've had all the horrifying Skype conversations I plan to have with Mom for the remainder of your childhoods. You will sit safely in the empty office, and then we'll go to the park together."

We found posters of *The Night Watch* and *Woman with Child in the Pantry*, and Dad paid for them. When we opened the big front doors of the museum, we could see that the steady rain from earlier had turned into occasional halfhearted drips.

"We might just see the sun today," Dad said approvingly as we boarded the bus. "I predict a delightful picnic later. Meanwhile, I expect you to use my meeting time as your own meeting time, while your memories from the museum are fresh. Over lunch I would like to discuss your potential plot and characters." We groaned.

The Dutch company Dad works for owns a building near the Westerkerk, one of the biggest churches in Amsterdam. The office is in an old canal house on the second floor. Just before we got off the bus, Dad pointed to a house on a corner where dozens of people stood in line. "That's the Anne Frank house," he told us. "Nine people hid there for two years during World War II. We can't go today, but I hope I can take you there before we go back home. Everyone should see it."

We followed Dad around the corner to an old brick house with a lime green door. He opened it, and we went right up the narrow stairway. At the first landing was another door with a sign that said SeaWind Corporation.

The inside of the office looked nothing like the outside. It was bright white and modern, and the only color in the room belonged to the woman sitting behind a sleek white and chrome desk. Her salmon pink cardigan and spiky, green-tipped hair definitely livened the place up. She hopped up from the desk when we came in and smiled at all of us.

"Hi Jeremy, so these are your kids?" she asked. "This one, with the cast—she's the little one who had the accident in the canal? You're Alice, right? I'm so glad you're okay!"

"That's Alice," Dad agreed, grinning. "Kids, this is Trees." It sounded like "Trace" when he said it, but the sign on the desk said "Trees Visser."

She saw me look at the sign and laughed. "Yes, my name is your English word for trees. In Dutch, two E's together say your A, so Trace, like Tracy."

Dad put his arm around me and his other hand on Milo's shoulder. "This is my older daughter Charlotte, who also took a dive in the canal the other day, and my son, Milo."

"Every Dutch kid falls into a canal sometime," Trees said, "but most of us don't do it quite so spectacularly." Alice gave her a modest smile.

"Can the kids sit in the back office while I'm meeting with Pim and Isaac?" Dad asked.

"Sure, absolutely," Trees said, and led us through a white and glass hallway past a half dozen doors. She stopped at the last one. "Make yourselves comfortable, kids. You'd like some tea, right? And some sweets or a stroopwafel? Have a seat." She gestured toward a stark white table with a half dozen twirly red plastic chairs pulled up around it. The chairs had black cushions on the seats. My mind was already writing a journal entry describing the chairs for Annabeth. They looked just like poppies. Alice plopped down and whirled all the way around.

"Be careful on those, kiddo, and don't break your other arm," Dad warned and walked to the door. "I'll see you three in about an hour, give or take a few minutes. I'll be in the conference room three doors down, but please don't interrupt unless you absolutely have to."

We were just getting our notebooks out of our bags when Trees kicked the door open with her foot. She had a tray in both hands and Milo jumped up to grab the heavy door before it swung back on her.

"Thanks," she said, putting the tea tray down on the table.

"I like your hair," Alice said boldly. "I've never seen anybody outside a book who had green hair. I think it's interesting. If your hair was long like mine, you could be a mermaid."

Trees laughed. "It's fun to do different things with it," she said. "Last year it was bright red, but I like to keep people guessing." Her clothes were feminine and almost, but not quite, traditional. The sweater had rolled roses on it; she wore a knee length skirt, and very high heels that would have been normal except they were turquoise.

"The bathroom's right around the corner from my desk," she informed us. "And if there's anything else you need, just let me know."

"I think we're fine," I said, "but thanks for the tea."

"And the stroopwafels," Alice said. The stroopwafels were already balanced on top of the tea cups, Dutch-style, and my mouth watered thinking about the caramel layer inside the cookie melting that very minute.

"Your dad's a genius. You know that, right?" Trees said. "I'm sure you already know that. At least, we think so. Everybody here is crazy about him."

I liked hearing her tell us that because I think things have been a little tense in the office in Boston, and that's part of the reason Dad wanted to leave early and come over here this summer. When the door closed behind Trees, we got very busy with the tea and the stroopwafels.

I pulled out my journal, wanting to write all about meeting Trees, and our second visit to the Rijksmuseum.

"Hey," Milo objected. "You can't do your journal now. We're supposed to be having a writer's meeting. Remember?"

"Dad's not really serious about this book thing, is he?" I asked. "I think it's like you said, Milo. It's not going to last. So what's the point?"

"I want to write a book," Alice said. "We might be famous. Maybe we could make enough money selling it to buy a house with a yard and a fence, and then I could buy my dog that looks like Jaap."

I shook my head. "We're not going to make any money, Alice, or be famous because we'll never finish it. Our book, if we write one at all, will be about five pages long. We've only got a month to do it."

"So we write as much as we can in the month," Milo said. He spun absently in his chair and looked out the window toward the houseboats along the canal.

Did Milo really want to do this? It almost seemed like he did. "You told Dad it was just a half-baked idea," I said.

"I know," Milo said, finally looking at me. "But I kind of got excited at the museum when we saw the same kid from your painting appear in *The Night Watch*. It's like it was meant to be. I wonder if anybody else ever noticed it before us."

"Don't forget my lizards," Alice said. "They have to be in the story, too, even if Charlotte's girl isn't at the park."

"Yeah," I conceded. "I admit the first two seem to go together. I know we can make something out of them. But the lizards are just strange. No offense, Alice, but I don't see how they fit into this story."

"But they're really the best part," Milo said, and Alice beamed as he continued. "I mean, nobody our age would want to read a boring story about two paintings from five hundred years ago. But everybody will want to read a story about how those guys in my painting turned into lizards. Zombie lizards."

"Huh?" I said. Trust Milo to add zombies to something serious like this.

He pretended not to hear. "The zombies terrorize Amsterdam. And maybe they keep coming back every few years. Maybe inside that little girl's teapot is a warning about how those Night Watch guys are going to turn into lizards if they don't do what the Spanish king says. Only they're not fazed by it; they decide to use it. They do turn into lizards, but they don't run into the canals and hide. They get bigger and bigger, and then they start wreaking havoc on the Spanish fleet. At first, the Dutch are as scared of the lizards as the Spanish are. Then they realize it's only their own watchmen, just changed into lizards, and they start helping them. They all fight together. When they win and once the Spanish flee like little babies, they turn back into men. But someday, someone's going to find that girl's teapot again, in an attic or an antique store, and the whole thing could just repeat itself. It isn't over."

This had all just sort of burst out of Milo, without a pause, and I stared at him with my mouth open. Alice's eyes shone. "Cool!" she cried. "Milo, you're a genius. I would totally like to hear that story at bedtime. It wouldn't scare me at all, since it turns out all right. It's better than Frances the badger."

I expected Milo to go on with more of the story, but he just sat there, staring out into the canal again, and I had to prod him back to the conversation. "So, are we going to write that down? Like an outline or something?"

"I'll do it!" Alice pulled her notebook out of my bag with her good hand, and laboriously, because her writing hand is broken, began to spell out "z.o.m.b.e.e.s."

"Thanks, Alice, but I can probably be a faster secretary," I said. Her face fell. She really wanted to feel like part of it. "Why don't you get started drawing some pictures of lizards?" I asked.

"I can hardly remember what they looked like, it's been so long since we've seen each other," Alice said sadly. Then she brightened. "That tree secretary out there seemed nice. Maybe she would do the work for us."

"I don't think we should ask her, Alice," Milo said. "She's already got a job."

"Okay, back up," I said to Milo. "Say that whole thing again and I'll write it down."

Right then we learned an important lesson, Writing a Book 101, and that's that you have to have your notebook and a pencil ready every minute because you never know when inspiration will strike. If you're not ready, you don't always get a do-over. Milo couldn't remember exactly what he'd said and kept forgetting details as we tried to piece it back together.

In the end, we took our new posters from the Rijksmuseum gift store out of their tube, and removed a few books off the floating bookshelf on the wall to weigh the posters down at the corners. We stared at the pictures thoughtfully.

"That girl is all golden in *The Night Watch*," Alice said. "She just sparkles. But why does a girl with such pretty clothes have a dead chicken tied to her waist? I don't get it." Alice and I both turned expectantly toward Milo.

"Um, let me think," he said, chewing his lip. "It looks like she's got some kind of pistol hidden behind the chicken, too. Maybe she just killed it, for their dinner?"

"Almost all of these guys have spears or guns," I said, looking over the scene. "But it's strange that the girl does, when she's so small."

"If I was in a big group of men with guns, I might want to have one, too," Alice said. "Especially since they don't look as though they're being very careful. A couple of them look like they're fooling around, and the chief guys in front aren't paying any attention, and they ought to be. The whole place might blow up."

"It's those two in the back whispering just to each other that I don't trust," I said. "The others look kind of dumb but harmless. Those two look like they might be planning something. I bet they're traitors. They're going to rat the Dutch out to the Spanish."

"Right," Milo said. "Should we have them turn into lizards like the others, or not?"

"Oh, they should be lizards all right," Alice said. "There aren't any Ten Commandments about killing lizards. When the other guys find out about them, how slimy they really are, they can take care of things while everyone's a lizard, and no humans will find out about it."

"We better write that down," I said.

"I've got a better idea," Milo said, taking out his iPod. "We'll record this conversation. Later, we can listen to it again if we need to."

"We've got to name the people," Alice said.

"We shouldn't name them when they probably were real people with real names already," I protested. "Maybe we should ask Dad if we can go back to the museum and find a book about the paintings. We can find out who the people were. We don't want to get things wrong."

"No," Milo said positively. "Dad told us to write a book, but it doesn't have to be an art history book. There's no way we could do that right. We're just kids, and it takes a long time to learn enough to write an art history book. Even if we spent years researching, we probably wouldn't learn anything new. We should keep it the kind of story we've been making up."

"We could name the girl Trees," Alice said. "She's got the wrong hair, but it's a Dutch name."

I shook my head. "No, I think we should make it a name that sounds Dutch, but would make sense to an American kid."

"I don't know very many Dutch names," Alice said, thinking. "Just Jacoba, like Mrs. de Hooch, but I don't want to name the golden girl that. It wouldn't sound respectful."

Milo had left the table and walked over to the bookshelf. "I'm checking the author's names for ideas," he explained. "Most of them are Dutch names, but I'm not sure whether they're men's or women's names, some of them."

Alice and I went over to help. I carefully took books off the shelves, passed them to Alice, and Milo wrote down the first name of each author. Some of them were clearly female: Elisabeth, Cornelia, Lottie, Lisa, Eva, Marijsa. Some, like Marcus, Hendrik, or Hanson were clearly male. But were Remmelt and Karel boys or girls names? Unpronounceable names like Grietje or Krisoijn we didn't even bother writing down.

We jumped when we heard a tap on the door. It was Trees. "Just checking on you, making sure you don't need anything else," she said. We backed guiltily away from the bookshelf.

"No, it's okay, absolutely, to look at the books," she said, "but I didn't realize you kids could read Dutch. I thought your dad didn't speak Dutch at all."

"None of us do," Milo confessed. "We just need Dutch names for a kind of a project we're working on together."

"For our book," Alice said, importantly. "We're writing one, and now we're trying to name the characters.

But since they're Dutch and we aren't, we're having a trouble finding good names for them."

"Does the book have anything to do with the posters here?" Trees asked, pointing to the table. We nodded. Milo looked a little embarrassed, but Trees seemed very interested when we related the basic plot to her.

"I haven't heard that theory before, the one about the paintings being connected," she said, looking suitably impressed. "When you get the story done, you should have it translated into Dutch. Many Dutch kids grow up going to the Rijksmuseum and looking at these two pictures, so they'd be interested. Amsterdam kids would love the tie-in from the lizards in the park. About the names, I can help you sort all that out. Let's get started."

"We don't want to keep you away from your job," Milo said.

"Oh, don't worry about it," Trees said, waving her hand. "It is a slow day, and I'm bored. What you're working on seems much more interesting than filing papers. How about I get my laptop and I'll help you type out some notes. I can send them to your dad, or print them out for you, whichever you'd prefer."

"Can we trust you?" Alice asked bluntly. "I mean, this is a really good idea that Milo had, and we wouldn't want you sneaking around like those two creepy men in the back of *The Night Watch*. You could sell our story in Dutch and we'd never find out about it."

"Alice!" I said, embarrassed. Trees grinned.

"You have my word," she said. "But if you'd rather, I can just write the notes down on a pad of paper. Then I will give it to you when you're done. See, no copies. But," she added mischievously, "it could fall out of your bag on the way to the train station, or a pickpocket might steal it, and your only copy would be gone forever. So there is a risk either way."

"I believe we can trust you," Alice said, spreading her hands out graciously.

"You two agree?" Trees asked Milo and me.

"It's fine," Milo said. "We know where you work."

"Great," she said. "I'll be right back."

We heard rapid clicking from her turquoise heels all down the hall. When she came back, laptop under her arm, she tossed a handful of wrapped licorice candies on top of the picture of the girl and her mother in the pantry. "Have some," she invited. "They're very Dutch, so they will help you get into the proper spirit."

Trees took notes much more efficiently than I had, and in what seemed like only a few minutes she had the basics of our story down. We thought of a whole lot more details as we did it, and she threw in a few good ideas, too.

"You need to know a little of the history going on at the time," she said. "I see you know that the Dutch fought Spain for independence, a bit like your country fought England for independence a few hundred years later. The Spanish were bleeding us dry, taking the best for themselves and the taxes were crazy."

"That does sound just like the American Revolution," Milo said, interested.

"And then, of course, there was religion," Trees said. "Spain wanted everyone here to be Catholics, but many of us were Protestant and wanted to stay that way. King Philip sent a duke to try to get the Dutch back in line. He was a horrible man, Duke Alva was, and tortured many people. Finally the Dutch couldn't stand it anymore and decided to get rid of Spain for good."

"So they went to war and drove them out," Alice said.

"It wasn't quite that easy," Trees said. "It took years, and even afterward, for a long time, people worried that the

Spanish would come back and try to take the country back again. So there were groups of soldiers in every town, called militias. They met, and did military drills, and probably even had some fun together sometimes. Later, even after they didn't need to worry about the Spanish anymore, the men kept meeting. By the time of the artist Rembrandt, these groups were like clubs."

"The lizards wouldn't have anything to do if we made this a true story," Milo said, frowning.

"Make it anything you want," Trees said. "I think Rembrandt and de Hooch would be honored just having their paintings in your story."

The door opened just then and Dad and two other men walked in. "Isaac, Pim, I'd like you to meet my children, Milo, Charlotte, and Alice," he said, and the men shook our hands.

"You look very busy," Isaac said, looking at the spread out pictures. "Studying the Dutch Masters?"

"No, Jeremy's kids are writing a book," Trees said, and she snapped her laptop closed. "I think they're off to a great start, and I predict it will be a best seller someday."

14

The Danger Point

After our picnic in the lizard garden, where Alice ran around trying to match up lizards with the right men in *The Night Watch*, we took the train back home to Ossenzijl. I was glad to walk in the front door. I always am.

It feels like home by now. I miss Mom, but I have to admit it's sort of fun to be the one who runs the house. I haven't had too many cooking disasters since the first one with the spicy noodles, and the house is so little, it's easy to keep clean. We've stuck to Mom's cleaning schedule pretty closely, but I have a feeling it still might not be clean enough for her.

I like to pretend that the house is really ours and always has been and always will be. I love to watch the rain drip off the thatch or the storks walking through the fields across the canal, and I love seeing all the blue and white pottery lined up in a row above the fireplace.

The painted brick walls of the house feel familiar and safe. Sometimes, when I'm reading downstairs, I look up at the skating medals hanging on the wall and pretend that Dad or Milo, or maybe even I won them. But who am I kidding? It would be more realistic to imagine that Grandma Sybil won skating medals. I can just see her, bent forward, zooming down a frozen canal with a determined look on her face.

There's a picture wall in this house, too, like the one we have at the apartment in Boston, but it's a twice as big, with loads of aunts and uncles and cousins. My favorite portrait is of a serious girl with a long, dark braid like mine. She's holding a bouquet of flowers and wearing her best dress, white with yards of lace. I made up a story about her for Annabeth, pretending this girl was our great grandmother. I want so badly for it to be true.

"I think we're getting to the danger point," I said to Milo one day the next week. We were sitting out on the dock fishing. We've been trying to fish half-heartedly all summer, but we haven't caught anything yet.

"What do you mean by danger point?" he asked, startled. He pulled his line up, frowned at it, and tossed it back into the canal.

"The danger point in a new place," I said. "You know, the point where you start caring about it. That's always bad if you know you can't stay. I guess I didn't think I'd get to that here. It's a foreign country and everything, and I knew we were only staying for the summer."

I kicked at the reeds next to the dock. "I was so mad when we left Kansas City, I didn't even *want* to like Boston until just a few months ago. But there are a few kids at church that I might make friends with, if we lived there longer. They finally started talking to me. I love having the ocean so close, and all the history around Boston is really cool."

"Yeah, it is," Milo said, after a long silence. "I don't know. I don't think I even tried to settle down in Boston. I just try to enjoy things as long as they last. And stand back a little."

That isn't enough for me anymore. I can't stand back a little, and I can't help loving it here more and more. Sometimes I just have fun doing whatever we're doing— bike trips with Dad, going to the store, getting hot chocolate, or having the freedom to go places without having an adult along every minute.

Then the truth hits me, and I remember. I don't live here, and in a couple weeks I'll be gone. I may never see this place again or the de Hooches. I think they're what I'll miss the most because we see them every day now.

Their house isn't showy like many of the houses in expensive American neighborhoods, but it's big for a Dutch house and interesting because they have things inside from places all over the world. One part of the living room is round, like a turret with long windows. All their souvenirs from Kenya are in there—some big drums that Alice likes to play on and a thumb piano. The dining room is full of Indonesian pottery and art. There are prints on the walls from their time in London, too. And of course, there are Dutch things everywhere. Some of them are old and some are new. Somehow it all fits together.

I felt a little strange the first time we went down for a real visit. Mrs. de Hooch had said we should come, but I wondered if she was just being kind after the accident. Mr. de Hooch was busy working on his boat when we got there, but he invited Milo on board to help him. He told Alice and me to go knock on the back door of the house and we did.

Mrs. de Hooch answered the door, all dressed up as usual but with a cleaning cloth in her hand. She smiled when she saw who it was. "Oh, hello," she said. "I didn't know if you would come or not, but I hoped you would. How is your arm, Alice?"

"Oh, it's fine," Alice said, holding up the blue cast. "A couple people from Daddy's work in Amsterdam signed it already. Will you?" She pulled out a marker from the pocket of her jeans.

Mrs. de Hooch hesitated a moment and Alice looked disappointed. "You don't have to if you don't want to," she said.

"Oh, but I do," Mrs. de Hooch said. She took the pen, and in small, neat handwriting wrote "Jacoba de Hooch" on the inside of Alice's arm by her elbow.

"Nobody will see it there," protested Alice. "And you're one of my most special friends here."

"You know that it is there, and that is the important thing, right?" Mrs. de Hooch said. She added a paw print right on top, and wrote Jaap's name too, which delighted Alice.

"Did we interrupt something?" I asked, pointing to the cloth. "Or can we help you?"

"I am just washing the front window," Mrs. de Hooch replied.

"Do you clean this big house all by yourself?" Alice asked, her eyes wide. "You're kind of old to be doing that, and you're dressed too nice."

"Alice!" I said, but Mrs. de Hooch smiled at me.

"It is all right, that she asked that," she said. "I do have a housekeeper. But she has plenty to do, and I like to do some of the work myself. It's a Dutch woman thing, cleaning. I am careful, and don't get dirty."

She showed us how she gets the windows perfect. She uses a small black squeegee, which we thought was great fun when we tried it.

"I'm going to do this back at our house," I said, remembering how streaked our front window looked compared with the other ones I've seen. Cleaning windows wasn't even on the chore rotation. I'd seen a squeegee in the laundry room. I just hadn't known what to do with it.

Mrs. de Hooch went back to another room and returned with a pile of filmy, starched lace. "The curtains," she said, and began threading them through a rod.

"You have curtains?" I asked, surprised. Now I could

see where they would go, right on the bottom of the window. Flower boxes of purple petunias and white alyssum spilled over with blooms outside. "Hardly anyone has curtains here, especially on the bottom," I said. "I've been noticing windows all summer."

"I like to feel that my house is my own," Mrs. de Hooch said, and I thought I might be prying too much if I asked why she worried about that when there was a gate around the whole yard.

When we finished hanging the curtains, she gave us tea and fancy gingerbread cookies. As we ate, she showed us a picture of her daughter, Marieke, with obvious pride. Marieke was tall and blonde, and Mrs. de Hooch must have looked like her when she was younger. In the picture, Marieke stood against an African mud fence with a gate. She wore a white linen blouse with sunglasses pushed up like a headband.

"Is Marieke married?" Alice asked.

"She is married to her job, I'm afraid," Mrs. de Hooch said. "Fortunately, she is very good at it. She takes after her father in that way. A good politician."

"I guess you have to be, to be in the United Nations," I said, and Mrs. de Hooch looked momentarily startled, then nodded.

"Yes, he had to be a good politician for that," she said.

"So you don't have any grandchildren at all?" Alice asked. "Not even one?"

"No, not even one," Mrs. de Hooch said. "It is very disappointing, but there it is."

"I wish we were going to be here longer," Alice said. "Because I think you would be a good grandma, and I only have one. But maybe we could pretend for right now."

I thought that was pushing it more than a little, since a

week ago, Mrs. de Hooch wasn't even speaking to us, and I decided it was time to take Alice home.

"Thank you for the cookies," I said. "And for showing me how to do the windows."

"Goodbye, pretend Grandma de Hooch," Alice said as she opened the door.

"It would be Oma, in Dutch," Mrs. de Hooch said.

"Really, she shouldn't say that," I began, blushing all over and trying to herd Alice out the door faster.

"Nobody has ever called me that before, and I think I would like to hear it for a few weeks," Mrs. de Hooch said. "You may both call me Oma, if you like."

"I hug my Grandma Sybil whenever I leave her house," Alice said, and she ran back inside and hugged Mrs. de Hooch. "So goodbye again, what was it? Oma?"

"Goodbye," I said, but I couldn't call her Oma and I couldn't hug her. Alice might be too little to realize she was at the danger point, but I'm plenty old enough to see it, and taking one look at Mrs. de Hooch I was pretty sure she knew it too. She smiled at me, though, and hugged Alice again, a little tighter.

"You squeeze really well," Alice said, approvingly. "Just like a real grandma."

Although I knew I shouldn't, I began to go to their house every day. I couldn't stay away. Mrs. de Hooch always seemed pleased to see us. Sometimes I saw Mr. de Hooch too, although in good weather he and Milo were usually out on the boat. Mr. de Hooch asked me to come along one day too, but I shook my head.

"I'm sorry, but I'm not sure I want to go. I know your boat is totally different from the rowboat, but whenever I think of being out on the water, I get a little nervous," I said.

"I understand," Mr. de Hooch said. "I'll ask again

later. You may change your mind. Give it a little time."

Walking home later, Milo said, "But Charlotte, you really ought to see inside the boat. They've got a little room with bunks, and a table and chairs. He said they go out for days sometimes, and sail into other countries, even." Milo's eyes clouded over. "I get why you might not want to go out in it, and that's my fault, but I wish you would. It's really safe. Mr. de Hooch is teaching me all about the sails. He wants to take us all out, even Dad, but it won't be fun for me if you can't go too."

"I want to go, but I don't," I said shortly, hating that an outing for the whole family hung on whether I went or not. "It's not just the boat; it's them."

"I think they're awesome," Milo said, surprised. "I thought you thought so too."

"I do," I said, "but they're getting too close. You're out with Mr. de Hooch every day. Alice calls Mrs. de Hooch Oma. She's teaching us to bake Dutch stuff and shows us pictures of when she was a little girl. It's not fair to them either, Milo. They don't have grandchildren, they probably never will, and they're pretending on us. That would be okay, but I really like them. I mean, I think I *really* like them, and we're about to leave, and we might never see them again."

"Or we might," Milo pointed out. "They travel all the time. He said he goes to the United States for meetings a couple times a year, even though he's retired. Maybe they would come to Oregon to pretend a little more out there." He grinned at me. "Just enjoy it. We never even met Dad's parents. You know I love Grandma Sybil, but she's the only grandparent we've got. She's great, but never makes cookies, and she sure doesn't sail."

"I don't want them for grandparents unless it's for real," I said. "I don't want to love more people in more places that aren't mine for keeps, that I have to keep leaving behind."

Suddenly anger bubbled up inside, at everyone and everything. We were almost home and I ran down the driveway and threw open the door to the shed. I grabbed my bike and got on.

I pedaled past Milo, who was still walking up the driveway, and didn't say anything to him even when gravel from the driveway spurted up as I flew by. I turned out onto the road and then out to the bike path, riding as hard as I could.

I couldn't look at the enormous, fairy tale farmhouses along the tree-lined road. I couldn't look past them to the ponies along the fence that Alice always wanted to stop and pat. I couldn't look down at the canal, perfectly calm and smooth today, or at my favorite little brick house at the end of the road, the one with the postage-stamp garden, every square inch covered in flowers. I couldn't look at any of it, because I wanted it all too badly, and it wasn't mine. Just like everywhere else where I started to feel attached, Ossenzijl didn't belong to me either. And now I loved it, and it was almost time to leave.

15

All Mine

I rode my bike hard for an hour before turning around, but by the time I got halfway home I'd stopped crying. I didn't have enough energy to cry anymore, and it took too much effort to ignore everything around me and still stay on the path.

I turned down the road next to a field not far from our neighborhood, one that Mrs. de Hooch told me had been carpeted with stripes of red, pink, orange, and gold tulips just a few months ago. I could picture it so easily, and it made my heart hurt. I wanted to see the tulip field blooming in real life, not just in the snapshot she'd shown me. I imagined the flowers alive and blowing, the orange tulips picking up the color of the farmhouse roof, the red ones matching the trim on the shutters, and I wanted them. I wanted the deep blue open sky above me to be mine. I wanted to bike down this tree-lined road every day, forever. I wanted it to belong to me.

Then a thought came so fast that I stopped the bike right there in the middle of the road. It did belong to me. It did. All of it was mine, and it always would be. The memories I have, my journal, the pictures in my mind—not just of this place but of Boston, and Kansas City and Oklahoma and Texas too—those really do belong to me, and I belong to them, for the rest of my life. Nobody can take it away, even if we move twenty more times. The only way I could lose them would be not to care or pay any attention. Someday, all the different places I know and love will be part of me, and they'll mix up together fine, just like the different things in the de Hooch's house.

I pedaled home, and this time I looked at everything, every lovely thing I passed along the way. It was all too beautiful not to look and remember for later. I soaked it in, and stored it up. Tonight I would draw pictures in my journal and write about it.

I got home just before dinner. Dad looked up from the computer. "I almost started to get worried about you," he said. "Milo said you were a little upset earlier. Want to talk about it?"

"Not really," I replied, hanging up my bag. The belonging feeling was too new to share with anyone, even Dad. Someday soon, I would tell him, but he loves going to new places so much, somehow I knew he must have figured this out for himself a long time ago.

"Well, I'm here in case you do want to talk," Dad said.

The computer made the burbling noise that meant Mom calling on Skype. Quickly, Dad leaned over to answer it.

"I have good news!" Mom said, when she saw us gathering around the computer. "Grandma Sybil's last treatment was today. She's threatening to start running again next week. I feel like I've been let out of jail."

"That's a week early," Dad said, surprised. "Are you sure that's safe, Meg? She was supposed to have one more week of chemotherapy."

"The doctor said he was positive," Mom said. "Her numbers are great, and he's confident they got it all with the surgery and treatments. She doesn't need radiation. I guess all that tofu and the marathons were good for something after all. I was thinking..." she said, and then stopped.

"I think I'm thinking the same thing," Dad said, grinning. "Come on back. I'll book you a ticket tonight."

"It's a lot of money just for a week, and last-minute ticket prices are so expensive," Mom protested. "It hardly seems worth it."

"What are you talking about?" Dad demanded. "Plenty of people go to Europe for just one week. We've all kind of settled in here, and you ought to feel like part of that. Besides." He checked behind him as if to be sure we really were all there. "I got a surprise this morning. How would you feel about not moving to Oregon?"

"Stay in Boston?" Milo said. "Man, I'd love not to move."

"But I was hoping for a house with a yard," Alice said. Her shoulders sagged in disappointment. "I don't want to stay in that apartment."

Dad didn't mean—he couldn't—but he was smiling like he had a secret he knew we'd all like.

"This project has gone really well," he said. "So well that they're offering me another contract, for a year this time. So if it's all right with you, Meg, you could fly up to Boston, pack up what you think we'd need in the way of clothes, send them over, and hire someone to put our furniture in storage. We're so streamlined these days that it shouldn't be too hard to do. We'd just stay here, and save the airfare of all of us going back and forth."

Alice was jumping up and down and Milo's grin practically split his face. It would only be for a year, but a year here? I thought about the bike ride I'd just got back from, the one where I cried for five miles straight because I loved it all so much and didn't want to leave. We wouldn't stay forever, we never did, but I wouldn't hold back this time. I would soak it all in. I would see the tulip field in bloom after all!

Then I saw Mom's face.

It's always been Mom's dream to live in Europe, and I thought she'd be thrilled about the offer. I think Dad was sure she would be, too, but she looked flabbergasted, almost as shocked as she had the day she'd gotten the texts about Grandma Sybil's cancer. And it didn't look like a thrilled kind of surprised at all.

The joy faded from Dad's face. "Is it your mother?" he asked, concerned. "You said she's doing great, but maybe it's not such a good idea to do this so soon after she's been sick in case she has a relapse. I can turn it down and I bet they'd have me again next year. Maybe that would be a better idea. Oregon isn't close, but it's closer than Europe."

"Mama's part of it," Mom began, but Dad interrupted her again.

"Is it homeschooling?" he asked. "We should probably think about that. We can't homeschool here; it's against the law and the kids would have to go to school. Christian schools are free, though. I thought school might be a good thing, just for a year. It would give you a little break and give them a chance to learn a new language."

"It's not that either," Mom said, and she started to cry. "It's what we always dreamed of, and I know you've enjoyed working for these people. But you see, I've found a house. And I want us to buy it."

"What?" Dad said, and I watched his jaw drop about two inches. "You've found a house? Why? Where?"

"Here, of course," Mom said, wiping her eyes with the back of her hand. "It's not too far from Grandma Sybil's. You've all seemed to love living in the country, and I found the perfect place. It's an old farmhouse on a couple acres. It was just renovated a couple of years ago. There's a creek behind it, and a barn..."

"My job," Dad said, flatly. "I mean, I guess I could get contract work and just fly out for it. But that means a lot of time away from all of you."

"Jeremy, you know all you have to do is call Phil, from your old company in Kansas City, and you'd have a job here," Mom said. "Not a contract, but a real job. One where we could stay put and stop moving every year or two. One where the kids could grow up going to every family holiday, and where their grandmother and aunt and uncle and cousins could be a real part of their lives."

"We call and Skype all the time," Dad said. "And visit, too."

"It's not enough," Mom said. "I don't know, maybe I'm having a mid-life crisis or something, but I just don't want to live like this anymore, going from place to place like nomads. I know you love the thrill of it, and you like the adventure of working different places and moving to a new town before the old one gets old."

She looked at all of us, kind of sadly, and added, "And I guess by now that's what the kids like, too. I'm sorry I ruined your big news. But we have to talk about this."

I thought maybe they were going to shoo us out of the room and hash it all out between them, but they didn't. Dad just sat there, silently, while Mom kept talking.

"There will be other houses. It's a great opportunity you've got over there. I can see that. It might be great for our family, too, for the kids..." She stopped.

"We wouldn't live here, would we, in this house?" I asked, trying to fill up the empty space.

"No," Dad said. "It's already rented out for part of September, and for December. And I don't think the owners would want to let it go for a full year anyway. Besides, if I take this job, I'd need to be closer to Amsterdam so I could go in more often. We wouldn't have to live right in the city, but I was thinking outside Delft or Leyden. Neither of them are long commutes from Amsterdam." His voice trailed off and it got too quiet again.

"So Oma and Opa wouldn't still be our neighbors," Alice said, disappointed. "But maybe we could come see them sometimes? And Jaap?"

I felt like we were torn between our parents, who both wanted us to choose their plan. My stomach hurt.

"I don't know what came over me," Mom said quietly. "I saw the For Sale sign in front of that perfect house, and I think I just snapped. I feel like this cancer thing was a wake up call. My mother is going to be all right—this time—but the next time she needs me, I don't know if I can bear to be so far away. I hardly know my niece and nephew. Your family doesn't seem to care to stay connected, Jeremy, but that's not the case with mine. I'll come to the Netherlands for a year, and I'm sure it will be wonderful. But after that, I want to come back here. I want to come home. To stay."

Alice, Milo, and I were barely breathing, waiting to see what would happen next. Finally Dad spoke.

"I'm going to turn this job down," he said. "And I'll call Phil in Kansas City. I'm not sure I can do it, stay in one place for years. He'll have to give me some flexibility."

He grinned suddenly. "He's going to have to let me take some contract work now and then, so we can go on more adventures like this with the kids. There's a wind farm in China that keeps pestering me to come over. I'd love for us all to go. Maybe we can make this work out somehow."

Without saying a word, Alice, Milo and I started to edge toward the door. Mom was smiling, but she looked like she was about to cry. "Thank you, Jeremy," she said. We could tell it was about to get embarrassingly mushy, and we all wanted to get outside before *that* happened.

I didn't know what to think or what to feel. None of us said anything until Alice stopped dead in her tracks. "A farmhouse, huh?" she said. "I bet I'm going to get a dog." And she took off down the driveway, singing and skipping at the same time.

16

Leaving

Mom came back three days later, on Alice's birthday. Alice bounced out of bed that morning, bounced into her clothes, and she sang on her bike all the way to the bus station.

> Happy birthday to me,
> Happy birthday to me!
> Happy birthday, Mommy's COME-ing,
> Happy birthday to me!"

When we passed another family taking a walk, Milo and I pretended we weren't related to Alice. I heard the song under her breath about a hundred times on the train before we got to the airport. I thought we'd never get there.

Alice, Milo, and I had made a big sign to hold up that said, "Welcome Back, Mom!" We wanted her to see it the minute she came into the arrivals hall. Dad kept checking the flight arrival board, and we knew when the plane landed, but we couldn't know exactly when Mom would get through customs and get to us, and our arms got tired from holding up the sign. Milo pushed through the crowd to get a better look through the big glass window, and he gave us a big thumbs up when he saw her coming through. We quickly put the sign up again, but I don't think Mom or anyone else could read what it said because in her excitement Alice kept jumping up and down, taking her end of the sign with her. When Alice saw Mom, she dropped the sign and ran toward her, pushing anyone aside who happened to be in her way.

Mom let go of her suitcase and carry-on bag, and somehow managed to grab Alice as she jumped into her arms. Dad got to Mom next, kissed her, and had started to do it again when Milo and I made it to them. Milo took the suitcase, and Mom transferred Alice to Dad and then hugged both of us at the same time.

"You all look wonderful," she said. "I can't get enough of you." Dad put Alice down and then took Mom's arm.

"You, on the other hand, look like you need someone to look after you," he said. Mom's brown hair was a little mussed up and there were dark circles under her eyes from trying to sleep on the plane. "For the next week, that's what we're going to do. You need a vacation."

"That sounds lovely," Mom said. "Trying to keep up with Grandma Sybil all summer wore me out. I could probably sleep the week away, but I'm not going to. Let me get a good nap, and then I want you to show me everything. And I hope I'll get to meet those nice neighbors you've been telling me all about."

"Oh, you'll meet them," Alice assured her. "They're coming for dinner tonight to help us celebrate my birthday." Mom looked alarmed.

"But don't worry," I said quickly. "You don't have to do a thing. We'll handle all the cooking, and we bought a cake from the bakery in town." The cake didn't look like an American cake with frosting on top because we couldn't find one like that. Alice's "cake" was actually a fancy apple pie with whipped cream on top. That was normal for Dutch birthdays Mrs. de Hooch had explained, so it was all right.

Mom looked relieved. "That's good," she said. "I'm

not sure I'm up to cooking for a dinner party the day of an international flight, but as long as you're doing the work, we should be fine."

"Our kids aren't bad cooks by now," Dad told her. "Charlotte burned steak last Thursday, but that's the only accident she's had in weeks. Since there weren't even any flames and we still ate the meat, I'm not sure we should count it. Even Milo makes oatmeal occasionally. And soup."

"From a package," Alice said, and ducked as Milo swatted at her.

"We're just kidding, Mommy," Alice said hastily. "We don't fight as much as we used to, either. I think we're mostly over it now."

"Well, that would make the whole summer worthwhile," Mom said.

"Isn't that the truth," Dad agreed.

We didn't go straight home but took the train to Dad's office to pick up some paperwork. Trees appeared to be doodling when we came in and she stuffed her pictures into her drawer. Today she wore shiny black pants that looked like they were made of snakeskin, and a frog-green sweater.

"Hello!" she cried, and jumped to hold the door open as we dragged Mom's suitcases inside. "How does the book come along, kids?" she asked.

"Not too great," Milo confessed. "We've got about twenty-five pages but it's kind of stalled."

"Well, you should keep going," Trees replied. "It's too good a story to quit."

"We're going to visit the lizards right after we leave here," Alice informed her. "It's my birthday and we're having a party there."

"Congratulations on your birthday!" Trees exclaimed,

and shook Alice's hand. "Maybe the lizards would like some party food too."

When we got to the park, Alice got busy right away tying shiny pink paper hats around all the lizards' necks, and we ate lunch perched on the brick ledge around the park. Alice put her arms around a monitor lizard with a particularly long neck, and Dad snapped her birthday picture.

"Time to take off their hats, kiddo," Dad said, when he finished. Milo and I helped Alice, getting about four hats for every one Alice took off. She wanted to give each lizard a personal goodbye.

"Who knows when I'll even see you guys again," she said sadly.

We went back to the office to pick up Mom's luggage and then on to the station. The first train we caught was almost full, and we couldn't get five seats together.

"Sorry, but I get Mom," Dad told us, and grumbling a little, we went down the car where there were two seats together and one across the aisle.

"It's going to be different, being a whole family again," Alice said once we were settled. "You've been a pretty good Mom, Charlotte. My hair doesn't have any big knots in it, and none of my clothes shrunk too much."

"Thanks," I said. "You've been a pretty good kid."

I thought about how strange it would feel to give the kitchen back to Mom and decided we would need to find a way to share it. Cooking is fun, and I really have improved because Mrs. de Hooch has taught me a lot during the last month. I can make two different kinds of cookies from scratch, and now I know how to make a Dutch roast and a special kind of mashed potatoes called *hutspot* that have onions and carrots in them.

"You can make this meal at St. Nicholas," Mrs. de

Hooch told me as we mashed the vegetables together. "It's a tradition."

"We've never celebrated St. Nicholas before," I said. "We're not big on traditions in our family."

"Well, you said your father told you his family is Dutch, so you are part Dutch," she said. "So it doesn't matter if you've done it all along or not. St. Nicholas is part of your tradition, and you can start it whenever you decide to. You can do it this year, on December fifth. You can make the roast, the *runderlappen*, we call it, and *hutspot*. You must put out wooden shoes, and in the morning, if you've been good this year—and if you warn your parents about what you expect—you will probably find oranges and chocolate coins, and maybe some presents."

I could picture it all in the new-old farmhouse, the spicy beef cooking on the stove, and Alice opening the door to the porch in the morning to find her souvenir wooden shoes full of oranges and chocolate. I could make gingerbread cookies, and hang them on ribbons, like I'd seen in some of the de Hooch's pictures. They did it no matter where they were, and in one of their pictures you can see African hills in the background.

"Although we did not leave the cookies out for long in Africa," she said, smiling. "The rats and bugs would have gotten them quickly. But we had to hang them, just for one night."

I made the roast and special mashed potatoes for Alice's birthday dinner party since it's the nicest thing I know how to cook. Most of the dinners we've made this summer started in a box. Dad isn't a bad cook, but between our lack of language skills and the fact that the cups and measuring spoon amounts are different here, it's just safer to go with a sure thing. For this special party, I wanted something better.

Alice and I set the table, wishing we had a nicer tablecloth than the thick plastic material, sold in rolls at the household store in the village. It's pretty, with birds all over it, but very informal, like the rest of the house.

"There isn't enough silverware," Alice said, worried. "One person will have to eat with their hands, I guess. That could ruin the party right there."

"We'll share one set," I said. "You can have the spoon, and I'll have the fork, and we can pass the knife back and forth."

"Okay," Alice agreed. "I guess that will work. But there aren't enough glasses either. I hope that Opa and Oma will not notice that you and I are drinking out of coffee cups."

"I'm sure they'll be too polite to say anything," I assured her, trying not to think about all the dinner parties they must have attended for so many years, with polished silver, shining crystal, and patterned china instead of thick, chipped, rental house dishes. But they'd seemed thrilled to be asked when we invited them.

"Of course we'll come," Mr. de Hooch said immediately, and Mrs. de Hooch beamed.

Later that afternoon, Mom got up from her nap. She looked a little bleary as she sat in one of the chairs and watched me cook.

"It seems strange to be having company coming in an hour and me just sitting here doing nothing," she said. I'm sure she was itching to get up and take over, but she restrained herself.

"It's going to be handy, having another cook in the family, though," she admitted, watching me brown the meat. She sniffed the air. "But Charlotte, are you sure you aren't supposed to turn down the heat on that roast?"

I dashed for a pair of tongs to turn the meat. Oh no.

The meat was a tiny bit burned on one side, but hopefully still edible. I stayed right next to the burner while I browned the other sides, and then turned down the heat, added water, and put a top on it just like Mrs. de Hooch had showed me. I chopped onions to add later.

"You've all grown up so much in just a few weeks," Mom said. "I'm trying to tell myself it's a good thing." Alice hopped onto her lap.

"I'm not too grown up yet," she said.

"Thank goodness for that," Mom said, and gave her a hug.

When Mr. and Mrs. de Hooch knocked on the door, dinner was mostly ready, although I'd misjudged how long it would take for the meat to cook. It needed a little longer even though the mashed potatoes were all ready and the bread and salad were on the table. I hurried to the door and opened it. Mrs. de Hooch held an enormous bouquet of yellow roses from her garden and Mr. de Hooch carried a package tied with a pink ribbon.

"Congratulations on Alice's birthday," she said, handing the roses to me. "Flowers for the cook, and a present for the birthday girl."

Alice ran into the kitchen and our guests kissed her on both cheeks and congratulated her. Mr. de Hooch handed her the gift. "Go ahead, open it now," he suggested, and Alice tore off the wrapping. When she found a stuffed dog inside that looked like Jaap, she squealed.

"Oh, thank you!" she exclaimed. "I'm going to teach him all kinds of tricks!"

"I hope he learns quickly," Mr. de Hooch smiled.

"How's dinner coming, Charlotte?" Mrs. de Hooch asked me.

"I'm not sure about the meat," I said, frowning. "It doesn't seem to be as done as it should be, and the potatoes are getting cold."

"Let me take a look," she said, and she was poking the roast with a fork when Mom hurried in, flustered because she'd been getting ready and hadn't heard our guests knock.

I knew they would all like each other, and I was right. Mom and Mrs. de Hooch talked about cooking and about moving around to different places, and she listened with interest as Mom told her everything about the farmhouse.

"How lovely for all of you," she said, admiring the pictures on Mom's cell phone.

Mr. de Hooch and Dad talked about traveling and technology. Dinner turned out all right. The meat was a little tough, but nobody mentioned it. We devoured every bite of the apple pie birthday cake. After dinner we played Uno, which Mr. and Mrs. de Hooch said they'd played with Marieke when she was little. Mr. de Hooch won. He played with an intensity that scared me a little, and I was glad his wife and Milo were on either side of him instead of me because he was a little too gleeful whenever he had punishment cards to play.

"Thank you for a truly memorable evening," Mr. de Hooch said, when they got up to leave. "I can't think when we've enjoyed a dinner party more."

Before they could go, Alice dragged Mrs. de Hooch over to admire the front window, which she'd decorated with a stuffed bear and groups of tiny plastic animals. It wasn't exactly the artful look I would have chosen, but it was Alice, all right. Thanks to Mrs. de Hooch's cleaning lessons, at least our window was as clean as any of the others on the street.

I still regretted the china and crystal we didn't have. "I'm sorry we couldn't make it nicer for you," I apologized.

"It was the very best kind of nice," Mrs. de Hooch said, smiling. "We wouldn't have missed it for anything.

You did an admirable job as hostess. Keep practicing in your new home." I told her I would.

For the next few days we took Mom to all our favorite places, like the windmills and the bakery, so she could try appelflappen, and even some not so favorite places, like the scary restaurant where we'd had the ice cream. None of us wanted to go in for another cone, but we all agreed that the place was so memorably awful Mom should see it. She took a picture of all of us in front of the building, grabbing our throats in mock terror.

The day before we left Ossenzijl, Milo and Alice went to see Mr. and Mrs. de Hooch one last time. I kept putting it off, finding things to pack or put away in the house. Really, I just didn't want to say goodbye to them.

"You have to go down there, you know," Milo said at suppertime. "They want to see you. I think they both feel bad you didn't go when Alice and I did."

After the supper dishes were finished and I couldn't put it off any longer, I walked down the road to their driveway one last time, and along the fence to the back yard. Jaap was outside and ran over to greet me, his black plumy tale waving. I patted him through the fence.

"Hey there, buddy," I said. He ran alongside me all the way to the back yard. The gate wasn't locked and I let myself in. I walked up to the terrace and knocked on the door. In a moment, Mr. de Hooch answered it.

"Good evening, Charlotte," he said. "We were hoping you'd come by tonight." Jaap bounded in behind me, straight through to the living room where Mrs. de Hooch sat embroidering. She looked up and smiled.

"I'm glad you waited to come," she said, snipping one thread and starting another. "I made these for your family, and they're just now almost done." I went over to see what she was making. On her lap were three Christmas ornaments, made of red and blue gingham with embroidered snowflakes on them. It took her about a minute to attach ribbons to the top so we could hang them on our Christmas tree. When she finished the last one, she handed them to me.

"They will pack almost flat, and I know that is important. They're to help you start your new Dutch traditions at Christmas."

"Thank you," I said, turning them over and examining the intricate stitching. "They're beautiful. I love them. We'll use them. Every year."

"We have really enjoyed having you as neighbors," Mr. de Hooch said. "Do you think maybe you might come back and rent the house again? We would love it if you did."

"Me too," I said. "I hope so, someday. Thank you for everything. I mean, it was the best summer ever, even with the accident, because of you, and..." The tears I'd been holding back all day started to spill out.

"We know what you are trying to say, Charlotte," Mrs. de Hooch said. "and you will always be welcome here."

I hugged them both and ran out the door. Jaap followed me down to the gate. I kept on running down the driveway, but he whined, and I went back to pat his head one more time.

17

It Can't Be True

The next day we left the house. Following the owner's instructions, Milo hid the key in the woodpile, and we bumped down the road, pulling our suitcases behind us. The suitcases were so full Dad said he was afraid we'd get charged extra at the airport, but there were so many things we couldn't leave behind. I kept looking back until I couldn't see the thatched roof of the house anymore.

After we'd dragged the suitcases on and off the bus and three trains, I realized Dad might have had a point about taking too much home. We were all tired and hot by the time the airline checked our bags and we went through security. Mom and Alice collapsed in the waiting area near our gate, but Dad, Milo, and I went into a bookshop to kill time before the flight left. "Don't even think of buying any more souvenirs," Dad warned us. "Your carry-ons are at full capacity. They shouldn't be asked to hold another thing."

Milo and I browsed through the magazine stand. He found a copy of *Sailing Life* and stood thumbing through it. I found a magazine with all kinds of funky Dutch-looking crafts. I wished I could find just a little more room in my backpack because I knew Annabeth would love the magazine.

Dad stood nearby, idly looking through the newspapers. Suddenly he snatched one off the rack. After a moment, he threw it down on the counter and paid the clerk for it.

"Dad, you said not to buy one single thing," Milo protested. "I've already read everything I brought with me this summer. I even read everything Mom brought. If you're buying a newspaper, can I get the sailing magazine?"

"Can I get the craft magazine?" I asked.

"Whatever," Dad said, tossing a large bill to Milo, who almost dropped it, he was so surprised. Dad hardly ever just hands any of us money. "But don't ask me to carry them for you."

Milo and I stared at each other as Dad left the shop. He sat down next to Mom and Alice, but didn't say a word to them. He was lost in the newspaper immediately.

"What was that all about?" I asked, and Milo shrugged.

"Search me. He bought a Dutch paper, too, and he can't even read it." Milo took the magazine out of my hand and paid the clerk for our selections.

"What's in the newspaper that's so interesting?" I asked Dad, once we sat down.

He looked up. "I'll explain later. I want to translate something on my phone before I lose connection." I looked over his shoulder but he closed the paper so I couldn't see it and smiled at me. "I promise, when I've got it figured out, I'll talk to you about it. But not now." I found a seat nearby and tried to be interested in my magazine, but I kept sneaking glances at Dad instead. He pretended not to pay any attention to me.

Even after we boarded, Dad was preoccupied. He handed the flight attendant the boarding passes and made sure we got settled in our seats, but then opened the paper and ignored us again. Alice and I sat next to a window, with Dad and Mom behind and Milo across the aisle. Every now and then I heard Mom and Dad talking in low voices behind me but I couldn't catch a word they said. It almost drove me crazy.

Finally, when I couldn't see the outline of the Dutch coast below anymore and the pilot turned the seatbelt sign off, Dad tapped me on the shoulder. "Mom's going to switch with you for a few minutes," he said, and she got up and moved next to Alice so I could sit down in her place. Then Dad handed me the newspaper. On the right corner of the front page was a picture of two men shaking hands. One of them was Mr. de Hooch.

"Not every girl," Dad said, "makes and serves dinner for a recent former prime minister of a European country, but you just did the other night." He smiled, enjoying my shock.

"No way," I said, staring at the picture. "He worked for the United Nations. He can't be the former prime minister, Dad. There aren't any bodyguards or anything. They have a maid, but do some things themselves. She washes her own windows! They're not—they can't be—"

I tried to read the writing in the article, but I only understood a few words and the ones I did know didn't help me. I saw Mr. de Hooch's name several times, but that was about all I got out of it. "What does it say, Dad?" I asked. "I just don't understand."

"Apparently he was at some ceremonial function the other day with a prince," Dad said. "That's where the picture was taken. He told you the truth about working for the UN, Charlotte, because he did, though he didn't tell you just how important that job was. And before that, he was the prime minister of the Netherlands."

"But like I said, there aren't any bodyguards or really anybody," I argued. "It just can't be true."

"Being prime minister of the Netherlands is an important job, but not quite like being president of the

United States," Dad said. "The Dutch are sort of a private, mind-your-own business kind of people, and besides, the royal family gets more press attention than the prime minister does. The de Hooches moved to Ossenzijl and just retired there. They didn't want any kind of fuss, and they didn't get any. Of course, it would never happen like that in America."

It still didn't add up. "What happened to them?" I asked, swallowing hard. "Because something did. Something awful. I never could ask what." I was thinking about Mr. de Hooch's leg, and how paranoid and rude Mrs. de Hooch had seemed when we first came.

"I had the same thought and checked it out on my phone at the airport," Dad said. "It was a freak thing. About a year ago he was visiting UN troops at a military base in the Middle East, and some local kids threw a grenade over the compound fence. He was just in the wrong place at the wrong time, which sometimes happens when you're visiting a war zone. I remember hearing about it now because it made headline news even in Boston. I can't believe I didn't remember his name."

I stared at the picture again. It was Mr. de Hooch in a way I'd never seen him before, with a tie and a tailored suit. I'd known without anyone telling me that he was an important man, but it hadn't occurred to me that he might be important to his entire country or maybe even the world.

"He was apparently a very popular prime minister," Dad told me, "and no doubt that led to his appointment to the United Nations. He had to retire after the business with the grenade. No wonder Mrs. de Hooch wasn't very pleased to see strange kids roaming around their private retreat."

"Why didn't they tell us any of this?" I asked.

I remembered the day we went to the hospital, the

special treatment we'd received and how respectful the staff was to him. I remembered how he'd chuckled when Alice wanted to take Jaap into the hospital. "We can probably get away with it," he'd said.

"I think they loved being anonymous with you," Dad said. "You didn't care about them because they were important. You didn't even know they were important. You just liked them, and they were there for you when you needed them."

"I feel so dumb," I said.

"Me too," Dad confessed. "We were all so ignorant about Dutch politics that not even his name meant anything. The only de Hooch you knew of was a Renaissance artist. It must have been a great deal of fun for them."

"They're pretty lonely, Dad," I said, and my throat burned and I was afraid I might cry right there on the plane. "They hardly ever see the only family they've got. They don't really have anybody."

"Many well-known people are lonely," Dad told me, and there were tears in his eyes too. "I'm sure the de Hooches have many friends from all the places they've lived, but those people are likely scattered all over the world and not close by. My guess is that the two of them are just tired of public life and want a quiet one. It's a good thing they have each other. I don't think he makes many public appearances, and one article I read referred to Mrs. de Hooch as 'reclusive.'"

"Do we tell them that we know?" I asked. "I mean, maybe we'll never see them again, but I said I would write."

"I wouldn't say a thing about it," Dad said. "If they wanted to talk about it, they'd have said something. Let them have what they need, some kids in their lives, and ones who aren't in awe of them." I decided he was right.

By the time the plane circled Kansas City, it was near midnight, European time, but I wasn't tired. Alice pushed next to me so we could both see the Kansas and Missouri Rivers, always our landmarks flying in. This was my city now. Tonight we'd stay at Grandma Sybil's un-air-conditioned house and probably nearly sweat to death before morning, but it didn't matter. Tomorrow the realtor would show us our new house. Home.

When we landed, I managed to jam the magazine into my backpack somehow, although it wouldn't zip all the way shut. I couldn't wait to see them all: Grandma Sybil with her new hair, Aunt Tracy, Uncle Jack, Anthony, who I hope has grown up a little bit from last year and won't pester me quite as much, and, of course, Annabeth. I had a moment of worry because Annabeth has so many friends. She was nice enough to include me all the time that year I lived in Kansas City, but we both knew that wasn't going to be forever. What if she didn't really want me to move here for keeps?

When we came through the doors, there they were, all of them. And strung between everybody was the biggest and most beautiful "WELCOME HOME" sign I'd ever seen. Each letter was poster-sized, in swirls and dots from a dozen different colors of paint. It must have taken Annabeth days to make it, but just like Alice had with the sign we'd made for Mom, Annabeth dropped her end, squealed, and ran to hug me. We shrieked together and jumped up and down, which was a lot harder for me than for her because of the backpack. When I bounced the last time, the backpack gave an ominous-sounding rip, and Milo managed to grab it just before the strap tore all the way off. It doesn't matter. I don't need it anyway. I'm not going to go anywhere for a long time.

18

Home

The new-old farmhouse felt like home right away. Unfortunately, the creek behind the house is too shallow for Milo to boat on, and the country roads aren't safe to bike on, but we've found plenty of other ways to have fun on the property. There's a barn out back, and we've got two goats named Jeeves and Wooster. They're Tennessee Fainting Goats, and whenever they get really spooked about something, they fall right over. I wish I could say we would never dream of doing that on purpose, especially Milo, who owns them, but that would be a lie. It's kind of fun to watch them go down. We always give them a good scratch behind the ears afterward. They're very forgiving.

Alice got her dog. Mr. de Hooch told Dad before we left that he wanted to buy her a Schiperkke puppy, and in October, we drove to a breeder in Arkansas to pick it up. All the way home, while the puppy sat curled up in each of our laps in turn, we talked about names for him. At first, Alice wanted to call him Jaap the Second, but finally she agreed on Wilhelmus, after the de Hooch's boat. We call him Wil, and he's the cutest dog in the world. Even though he belongs to Alice, I've done most of his training, and he loves me as much as he loves Alice. Wil comes, heels, stays, and can sit up and beg. Alice says he's just as smart as Jaap. I think he's even smarter.

A few weeks after we moved in, Annabeth came along with Mom and me to the paint store to help me pick out a color for my new room. I chose one called Aerie blue, and it looks really light and peaceful in the morning and darker at night. When the light hits it in the afternoon, my room turns the same color as the sky on a sunny Dutch day. Once we got it painted, Annabeth helped me put all my stuff away. Mom bit her tongue and didn't say anything about the five posters I hung up as soon as the walls were dry enough, or the piles of papers I tossed on the shelf in my closet. I love knowing they're going to be up there long enough to get dusty someday.

"Ow!" Annabeth cried, as a thick folder fell off the pile she was lifting to the shelf. Papers scattered everywhere. "What's this?"

It was my copy of *The Lizard Garden*, which of course we never did finish. I was right about that, although we did get a lot farther than page five. There were twenty-six double spaced pages on Dad's computer by the time we went home. Every few weeks, Milo nags me to work on it again, but so far we've never gotten around to it.

On December fifth, St. Nicolas Day, I was in the kitchen showing Mom how Mrs. de Hooch taught me to make runderlappen and hutspot when Alice came running down the hall and into the kitchen, waving a package.

"It's for you and me and Milo!" she cried, breathing hard. "And it's from the Netherlands!"

"The de Hooch's?" I asked, wiping my hands on a towel.

"Nope," Alice said, squinting at the return address. "It's from that Tree lady at Daddy's office."

What would Trees be sending us? "Go get Milo," I told her. "I think he's out with the goats." Alice grabbed her coat from the rack by the door and dashed out to the pasture.

The package was thick and flat, and while I waited for

Alice and Milo to get back I slid a knife along the seam, and just sort of felt around inside.

"Hey, no fair peeking, Charlotte," Alice protested when they came in. "It's addressed to all of us, not just you."

I pulled out a wrapped package. On the top was a note. Milo snatched it out of my hand.

"Read it out loud!" Alice demanded.

"*You were wrong about me*," Milo read. "*I am both a thief and a liar. I emailed your father several months ago and asked him if you were still working on your story. He said no, that you had abandoned it completely. I think it's far too good for that, and since I'm a starving artist when I'm not a secretary, I made some illustrations to go with the story. A publisher friend seems to like it, and it's going to be made into a book here in the Netherlands sometime next year. Don't worry, I'm not such a thief that I won't give you credit. Our names will all be listed as co-authors, with mine as illustrator. I'm sending you copies of some of the pictures I've made so far. I hope you approve.*"

Alice put her hands on her hips, outraged. "Well, of all the nerve," she exclaimed. "I cannot believe she did that without asking us."

Carefully, I opened up the bundle of drawings Trees had sent. She'd made it a picture book, not the novel Milo and Alice and I had started to write. Since she meant it for little kids, the story was funny, not scary. The soldier lizards were busy getting into all kinds of trouble all over Amsterdam. Trees had reproduced the settings of the paintings in brilliant color, as though they were coming to life, while the lizards were just thick brown outlines scuttling across the page. Somehow, it was all warm and full of life.

"Man, she's good," Milo said, admiring a drawing in which several lizards had commandeered a sailboat on a canal and tied up a terrified Spanish captain. "Trees isn't going to be a secretary very long, I don't think."

Looking through the pictures, I had to agree. I bet *The Lizard Garden* is going to sell really well. I'll be thrilled if it does, but I feel proud just thinking about Dutch kids enjoying our story. We couldn't stay in the Netherlands, but something we helped to create will go on making kids happy there.

And I'm happy too. Right here, where I belong.

Acknowledgements

Until I wrote a book of my own, I had no idea how profoundly unfair it is that only the author's name appears on the cover. So many other people contribute to a story becoming a book.

Many thanks to Barbara Coyle and Carol Shell, who edited the manuscript. Amy Kate Hilsman and Pam Johnson each helped proofread and edit sections, offering advice and encouragement. Chautona Havig spent many hours formatting the manuscript for publication and creating the beautiful cover. I hope that one day I can help another beginning author as much as she's helped and encouraged me.

To my supportive family who not only understood the time I spent working on this story, but cheered me on, cooked meals, made coffee, and offered many excellent suggestions on wording and plot—this story belongs to you, too. I love you, and thank you.

While the plot of this story is fiction, the places are real. The lovely little Dutch town of Ossenzijl and its sister village, Oldmarkt, are located in the province of Overijssel. (You can visit the Café Vanhandel, though I don't recommend it.) The lizard garden is real.

Made in the USA
Charleston, SC
20 February 2015